NO TEARS FOR MASSA'S DAY

NO TEARS FOR
MASSA'S DAY

Michael Humfrey

JOHN MURRAY

FOR NICK DAVIES

First published 1987
by John Murray (Publishers) Ltd
50 Albemarle Street, London WIX 4BD

Typeset by Inforum Ltd, Portsmouth
Printed and bound in Great Britain
at The Bath Press, Avon

British Library CIP data

Humfrey, Michael
No tears for Massa's day.
I. Title
813 [F]   PR9265.9.H8

ISBN 0-7195-4442-4

Part One

I

The island of Saint Cecilia lies at the centre of the Caribbean Sea. On a detailed map of the West Indies its elliptic shape is neatly quartered by the intersecting threads of the 78th meridian and the 15th parallel. Not far to the north is Jamaica, less than five hundred miles to the south the Panamanian isthmus; inevitably, it was this favourable position, with all the strategic advantages it conferred, that led the Spanish, the French and the British at various times to spill each other's blood for possession of the place. During the first half of the eighteenth century Saint Cecilia changed hands seven times, and the wrangling was not brought to an end until the Treaty of Paris finally ceded the beautiful island to the British Crown in 1763.

Robert Langford and his family arrived in Saint Cecilia on the first day of March 1779. The Dutch ketch in which they had found passage from Grenada made landfall at the eastern extremity of the island as dawn broke; in the un-defiled, diamond light the island shimmered like a jewel in its cobalt setting. For the rest of the morning they sailed before the south east trades along the southern coast. The ill-fitting vertebrae of the cloud-draped spine of the Blue Mountains rose up from the centre of the island and, from the foc'sle of the ketch, Robert could see that the coastline was indented by a succession of bays and inlets. At the head of each of the larger inlets, an untidy aggregation of clapboard bungalows had sprung up behind a wooden jetty and a little cluster of merchants' shops and shingled warehouses.

Where the land sloped down from the base of the

7

mountain range to the sea, and again in the broad river valleys, the neat, familiar, cross-hatched pattern of sugar cane fields extended almost to the water's edge. Close inshore, a flotilla of plumb-stemmed trading schooners moved purposefully from one small port to another, their triangles of weathered canvas starkly silhouetted against the green backdrop of the land behind them. At the head of one of the larger inlets, Robert identified a pair of tall West Indiamen out of Bristol or Liverpool. They were hoisting aboard hogsheads of raw sugar from a fleet of flat bottomed lighters ranged alongside like piglets at their mother's teats.

From time to time, as the Dutch ketch passed along the coast, it was possible among the fields of cane to make out the whitewashed, colonnaded facade of some wealthy planter's Great House, with the up-raised finger of its nearby factory chimney spewing a thin column of ash into the air. At intervals between the fields, a single poinciana tree erupted in a cascade of scarlet blossom. The ketch made good time through the water, hauling behind her the ephemeral tail of her narrow wake.

Robert Langford sat a little distance apart from his wife and two children, as if unwilling to share with them the crushing burden of his own sense of loss and the conviction that, for whatever reason, God had abandoned him. He watched in silence from the deck of the vessel as the coastline of Saint Cecilia passed in review, too preoccupied with his own misery to find the smallest degree of pleasure in anything he saw. Even the rich green fields of cane were to him now merely a bitter reminder of what had been taken from him; their well-tended appearance stirred only feelings of envy, not of admiration.

A thin tongue of spray, flung up by the bows of the ketch, was caught by the wind and struck Robert lightly on the face. He put up a hand to wipe away the warm salt water; then, in case one of his children should look round at that moment and misunderstand the wetness on his cheek, he deliberately turned his back on his family and walked towards the bows of the ship. There, concealed by the bulk of the capstan, his large frame braced against a rusting anchor, his red-rimmed eyes fixed unseeing on the distant horizon, he sat alone on the deck with his thoughts of what might so easily have been.

Robert Langford was the third generation of his family in the West Indies. His grandfather, Cleydon, had arrived in shackles as a hapless rebel more than ninety years before, transported to Barbados for life from his nameless village in the west of England. Cleydon was no more than a boy of seventeen at the time, but he was taken at Sedgemoor by the King's soldiers with a pitchfork in his hands and he was considered fortunate after his trial to have escaped with his life.

He served his ten year sentence at hard labour on a sugar plantation to the east of Bridgetown where, unlike most of those who had been sentenced with him, he managed to survive both the murderous heat of the tropical sun and the malignant attentions of the white overseers in the cane fields.

After his release, he eked out a living as a fisherman on a deserted Barbadian beach in the company of a kitchen maid from the hated estate, whose own period of indentured service had expired at the same time. The woman bore him several children, but only one – a son called James – lived beyond infancy.

Cleydon and his woman died within a month of each other when the boy was fourteen. With nowhere else to go, James Langford found work as a groom on the same estate his parents had once been bound to, and he was to remain there, obedient and unassuming, for the rest of his life. In 1735 he married the daughter of the Head Cook at the Great House. Robert Langford was their son.

Unlike his father, Robert Langford was never satisfied with the prospect of spending his life as a servant on another man's land: with an intense, almost mystical passion, he craved land of his own. The craving caused him to leave the security of the estate on his sixteenth birthday. For three years he had been apprenticed to the estate cooper, but he chafed at the monotonous task of fitting the broad oak staves into their metal hoops and, in the end, his master was glad to see him go.

Robert found work first as a logger on the wet, malarial coast of Honduras; the land on which he felled his trees was not his own, but at least he laboured only for himself and the Spanish government, which owned the territory, did not seek to displace him. Then, in 1764, the chance for which he had prayed suddenly presented itself: the island of Grenada, neighbour to Barbados, passed unexpectedly to the British Crown by the terms of the same extortionate Treaty with the French that also ceded Saint Cecilia. In London, the king offered ten acres of Grenadian soil to any British subject willing to clear the rain forest that cloaked it. Abandoning his felled logwood trees where they lay in the Honduran mud, Robert Langford was one of the first men to take advantage of the king's offer.

He did well in Grenada. His grant of ten acres lay in a fertile river valley. He arrived there late one September afternoon to take possession of his land and he fell to his knees and thrust his fingers deep into the earth, grasping the rich, damp soil in both hands so tightly that the moisture oozed out between his fingers in thin rivulets of mud.

Not far from where he knelt on the grass, the river cascaded over a ledge of rock into a bright circle of water. He looked down at the rich earth in the palms of his hands and the music of the falling water seemed to echo the words in his heart: this is my land, at last my own land. For the rest of his life, he never forgot the joy of that magical, unrepeated moment.

He quickly tamed his property. By the end of the first year he succeeded in replacing the tangled bush with orderly ranks of sugar cane; and in the following year he married the widow of the Englishman who had worked the holding beside his own and who had been taken by cholera while on a rare visit to the capital. The woman's name was Agatha and her plot of land was fused with Robert's to form a single property of twenty acres whose northern boundary was the river. The sugar cane flourished in the rich alluvial soil and, in Europe, the price of sugar doubled and then doubled again. At harvest time, he had been obliged to hire labour to reap the cane and, at the end of the thirteenth season, it was possible to talk with his wife about the day when they would build their own small sugar factory on a spur that overlooked the river.

Providence, however, did not permit it. In 1779, while the British Government in London was preoccupied with the rebellious American colonists, the French took advantage of their old enemy's discomfort to recover Grenada for themselves. The invading soldiers swept over the island, burnt down Robert's house and confiscated his land. With his wife and two young children – and with what little money the soldiers had failed to discover beneath the mud floor of his bedroom – Robert fled to the capital and sought refuge on board a Dutch ketch bound for the only remaining place in the Caribbean where grants of virgin land were still available to British peasants – the island of Saint Cecilia.

Now, with the rust-stained fluke of the vessel's spare anchor pressed hard against his back and the wet, unyielding deck beneath his buttocks, he sought again the answer to the question that had plagued him throughout the seven days of the voyage from Grenada: what had he done to merit so severely God's displeasure?

In the middle of the afternoon they took in sail and the ketch threaded its way through a treacherous maze of white sand cays and the shifting shadows of coral outcrops; then, with an abrupt change of course, the vessel passed from the open sea into the protected waters of Queenstown, the island's capital. The entrance to the harbour was guarded by the cannon of a star-shaped fort which stood at the southern extremity of a long spit of coarse grey pebbles. A weather-stained naval frigate rode at anchor in the shadow of the fort's granite walls; after the fall of Grenada, the threat of a French invasion hung like a sombre shadow over the small British garrison.

From his place in the bows, his long legs thrust out across the deck, Robert watched as the ketch followed the tortuous course of the ship's channel. The tide was running out and on both sides grey-green beds of eel grass were exposed to the searing heat of the afternoon sun. The decaying wreck of a dismasted schooner lay in the grip of an advancing forest of mangroves. The drying mud of the eel grass beds emitted a cloying, sulphureous stench. The prevailing wind had deserted them at the entrance to the harbour and the faded Dutch tricolor hung limp against its flagpole at the stern.

They tied up an hour later alongside one of the several wooden jetties which thrust out into the sluggish water of the harbour like a cluster of probing fingers. Robert rejoined his family on the foc'sle and together they looked about them at the town. It was a place of contrasts. The ornate, pretentious houses of the wealthy Cecilian merchants stood on filthy, rutted streets within easy reach of their places of business on the waterfront. Rising from the centre of the town the shingled, needle spire of a church was starkly silhouetted against the blue faience of the sky behind it.

Many years ago, the town had been laid out on a regular pattern with a main north-south axis, but it was apparent to Robert as he stood on the deck of the ketch that, as it had grown and spread away from the sea up the gentle slope of the alluvial plain on which it stood, the original pattern had become a casualty of every merchant's determination to build himself a finer house than his neighbour's. The plots of land grew successively larger and more irregular in shape until the new roads leading north from the town were forced to twist and turn along whatever untenanted strips could be found for them.

On the waterfront, a small crowd of anxious merchants waited to interrogate the passengers as they stepped ashore from the ketch. The British frigate anchored in the shadow of the fort had brought news of the loss of Grenada only the previous day, and the Dutch vessel was the first ship to arrive in Saint Cecilia bearing people who could give a first hand account of what had happened.

Many Cecilian families had relatives among the planters of Grenada, and some of the more adventurous merchants had hastened to invest money there when the island passed into British hands fifteen years earlier.

A stout businessman, sweating profusely in a brocaded purple waistcoat, caught Robert by the arm.

'I own property in Grenada', he announced. 'Are those French devils confiscating everything there now?'

'I only know they took my land,' Robert replied wearily.

'I have a chandlers place in the capital,' the man said, tightening his grip on Robert's arm. 'I must know if they have taken it.'

Robert shook himself free.

'I cannot tell you', he replied. 'I did not stay to see.'

'It was on the waterfront,' the man continued. 'You must have passed it when you boarded your vessel . . .'

But Robert had no stomach for another man's troubles; his own were more than sufficient. Ignoring the man's protest, he led his family along the pitted road towards the centre of the town. They walked past a file of open-fronted rum shops, each with its clientele of drunken seamen sprawled upon wooden benches set just out of reach of the afternoon sun. The harbour was full of ships and there was a vessel alongside each of the several wooden jettys; the discord of loud, peremptory voices directing the loading and unloading of cargo was overlaid by the persistent high-pitched squeal of complaining pulleys. The children

13

whimpered, bewildered by the unfamiliar press of people and still suffering the effects of the motion of the ship which had brought them so far, and so unexpectedly, from the familiar security of their Grenadian river valley.

Robert carried the family's travel-stained canvas bag in one hand; the other strayed from time to time to the money belt at his waist. The belt contained twice as many silver coins as he had brought to Grenada with him fifteen years earlier to start a new life there, but at that time his only responsibility had been to himself; now he had a wife and two children to support and the coins would be few enough for that purpose. He was suddenly weighed down by an indescribable weariness of spirit at the thought of having to start all over again; then the needs of the moment reasserted themselves. He straightened his back and sought directions from a passerby to the office which allocated land to new settlers like himself. He reminded himself that he had done it all once before; it could only be easier the second time around.

There was no lack of empty land for settlement on Saint Cecilia. The island was many times the size of Grenada and it still contained fewer than two hundred thousand people, nine-tenths of whom were slaves. But the land set aside for distribution to peasant settlers was indifferent. The fertile valleys and rich alluvial plains, which they had all seen from the deck of the ship, had long ago been claimed; and for their owners they had produced over the years the fortunes which in turn gave rise to the fine, colonnaded Great Houses that the family had noticed among the fields of cane.

At the Land Office, Robert was offered two quite different plots on which to settle. The first lay on the mountain slopes far to the west – wild, fertile, uncleared rain forest which, from the clerk's brief description, sounded not unlike the kind of land Robert had tamed in his Grenadian valley; the other sprawled along the south coast at the mouth of a river, flat, low-lying and cloaked by a thin covering of scrub.

Only a few weeks earlier, faced with the same choice Robert would instantly have demanded the rich, wild land in the hills, but the spirit had been sucked out of him. He could no longer face the prospect of having to clear wooded land with no slaves to help him and his children still too young to swing an axe.

With a troubled soul, he chose the land by the sea.

The clerk fetched down from a shelf of his office a crude map of the southern coast. With an ink-stained finger he pointed to an area marked as Treasure Bay.

'The land is there,' he said, 'to the west of the river bordering the sea. You may stake out as much as you can cultivate. For the time being, the Assembly has set no limit on it.'

Robert was instantly suspicious. 'Why is that?' he asked sharply. 'Do people not care for that land, then?'

'Who can tell?' the clerk replied evasively. 'It is at least well watered. Of course, if you do not wish land of your own there is always labouring work to be had on other men's estates.'

But that was an option which Robert could not bring himself to face.

'I will take the land,' he said.

A large, leather-bound register lay open on an easel next to the clerk's desk. The man stood up and with some effort entered Robert's name on a fresh page of the register. Then he returned to his desk and made out the Deed of Ownership on a small sheet of pale brown paper.

As the clerk's quill scratched across the paper, Robert examined the map. With a blunt forefinger he traced the shortest route from the capital to Treasure Bay, committing it to memory. He reckoned that the total distance would be a little more than sixty miles. At one point the black thread of the road was intersected by the wavering blue line that indicated the course of the river from its uncertain source in the foothills of the central mountain range down to the sea. At other similar places on the map the word 'Ferry' had been inked in, and at one important junction a bridge had been sketched over the blue line of the river; but at the place where the road they must follow met the river they would have to cross, there was nothing written on the map.

The clerk completed the Deed of Ownership and handed it to Robert, who placed it within his shirt; then Robert strode out of the soft light of the Land Office into the harsh afternoon glare of the waterfront. There was a sudden gust of wind; on the glassy surface of the water the reflected image of the sun was shattered into a thousand separate, quivering mirrors. The shafts of light stabbed painfully at his eyes. His wife and children were waiting for him where he had left them in the shade of a giant saman tree beside the customs house. He pulled the Deed out of his shirt to show them.

'We have land again,' he said, but somehow his heart was not in the words and the moment passed without any sense of joy.

Robert's first task was to use some of the precious silver coins in his money belt to buy the tools that they would need to work their new land. He bought them from a dry goods store beside the church with the needle spire, and from the same place he purchased a long-backed, raw-boned mule which was penned with several other animals in an enclosure at the rear of the premises. Finally, he sent Agatha with the children back to the open market they had passed on the waterfront to buy food to see them through the next few days on the road to Treasure Bay.

They slept that night in the graveyard of the church, with the mule tethered to a stake at the margin of the consecrated land. Robert roused them at first light and they set out at once on the road that led north from the capital. They had been walking for about three hours when they arrived at a crossroads and, recalling the map he had studied in the Land

16

Clerk's office the previous day, Robert led them westwards. From this point onwards, the road on which they travelled became little more than a bridle track carved out of the vigorous, encroaching bush. The family was forced to pass in single file, the children perched on the mule's long back while their parents took it in turns to lead the unwilling animal.

The coast was soon left behind them and they began to climb into the rugged, broken foothills of the central mountain range. The air grew perceptibly cooler and the characteristic vegetation of the plains gave way to larger, more exotic plants. Barrel-trunked guango trees, the great branches festooned with bearded epiphytes, towered over them. Huge ferns and thick stands of balisier with brilliant scarlet bracts sprang from the brick red soil. Serpentine lianas bound each tree to its neighbour and hung down in loops towards the forest floor. Only an occasional shaft of milky sunlight pierced the moist gloom beneath the canopy of leaves. When night came, they slept exhausted among the buttress roots of a silk cotton tree and were not woken by the rain that fell in the hour before dawn.

During the afternoon of the second day of their journey, they found that the track they were following abruptly swung towards the south; by sunset they had left the foothills behind and were once again entering the broad plain of the southern coast. They camped that night in a fold in the earth beside the track. There was a grove of coconut palms nearby and, by the light of an early rising moon, Robert climbed one of the trees and twisted the heavy green nuts from the trunk. They drank the sweet water and, when that was gone, Robert used one of the new cutlasses he had bought to slice open the nuts and reveal the soft white jelly inside. The night was cold; when they had eaten the coconut jelly, they slept huddled together in their fold in the earth to gain what comfort they could from the warmth of each other's bodies.

Next morning, not long after they had set out again at dawn, the track widened without notice in front of them and they found themselves for the first time passing through cultivated land.

The land was planted with sugar cane. There were no hedges to separate the fields, only narrow, grassy intervals just wide enough to allow a laden donkey to pass by when the cane was harvested. In one of the fields, close by the road on which the family was travelling, a gang of naked black slaves was bent over the rich earth of the plain, tending the needs of a new generation of cane. The men and women laboured together, their children at their sides or strapped to the backs of the women; behind them stood another Negro entrusted with a different task. This man wore a pair of ragged pantaloons as a badge of office and he carried in his hands a long leather horse whip; and whenever one of the slaves paused in his work to straighten his back or to wipe the sweat from his face, the whip snaked out and coiled around his bare torso. Not far away a white overseer patrolled the fields on horseback, carrying a leather lash of his own to strike in turn the pantalooned Negro whenever he proved too sparing in the use of his whip.

The road through the sugar plantation was paved with crushed limestone; a fine white dust rose from their feet and clung to their sweating skins. A little party of slaves was walking ahead of them on their way to another section of the estate, and Robert's children watched in fascination as the colour of the Africans faded from polished ebony to a sickly, indeterminate grey, except where the sweat carved black rivulets through the limestone dust on their naked backs.

The heat of the morning rose in trembling, quivering waves from the surface of the road; the fine dust parched their throats. They passed a pair of ornate limestone gate pillars inscribed with the name of the property through which they were travelling. Beyond the wrought iron gates the estate driveway ran in a dead straight line for about a quarter of a mile. The driveway was flanked by a double row of royal palms; the smooth, grey trunks soared into the air like the columns of some ruined tropical temple, bursting at the top into green circlets of feathery leaves.

The family stopped to look. At the far end they could see that the driveway opened abruptly on to a cobbled square, at the back of which stood the sugar factory. The factory was laid out on the gently sloping spur of a hill. About two hundred yards above it was the gabled Great House where the Master and his own family lived, and from where he could look out over the extent of his land whenever he chose and be satisfied that his slaves were not wasting a single minute of the day.

Between the Great House and the factory there was a scattered collection of mean little bungalows occupied by the white overseers; and on the level beneath the factory were the slave lines with their crude mud and wattle huts and their little back yards, each with an open hearth and a metal cauldron standing beside it.

Not far from the slave lines, Robert noticed a herd of brown cattle grazing in a pasture. There was a muddy pond lying in a natural depression in the middle of the pasture and some of the animals had ambled into the shallow water to escape the heat of the day. The small black boy who had charge of the cattle picked up his staff from the edge of the pond and waded in to fetch them out. His high-pitched words of command echoed over the fields as the animals reluctantly hauled themselves out of the water. From his chest to his feet, the boy's naked body glistened with a cloak of mud as he followed the cattle on to dry land.

Beyond the pond, a rectangular field had been divided into a large number of equal squares like a draughts board. Robert recognized it as the slaves' provision ground, where they would spend each Sunday tending their plots of soil to grow the food which kept them alive. It had been done in just that fashion on the Barbadian estate where he was born and, in a curious way, he had envied the slaves those small squares of soil which they had been able to treat as their own . . .

The mule grew impatient and threatened to break loose; the family moved on again. The road swung to the left; in a field beside it another gang of slaves was excavating a shallow irrigation ditch. Some of the men were singing softly to themselves as they worked, sad, rhythmical, repetitive chants which they had brought with them from the forests of the Guinea Coast.

The sight of the naked Africans bent over their work reminded Robert of a story his father had once told him about his own father, Cleydon: when Cleydon Langford had arrived in Barbados in his convict's shackles, he had never seen a black human being before. The ship's agent had come aboard in Bridgetown harbour accompanied by two personal slaves; as one of them turned to assist his Master at the head of the ladder, Cleydon had been astonished to discover that it was not true, as he had been led to believe, that Africans possessed short tails.

The memory of that story brought back to Robert, too, his father's own vivid recollection of the slave rising which had taken place on the Barbadian estate where he was born. The rising had begun on New Year's Day in 1746. It had been planned and led by a giant Mandingo called Kofie and it failed only because a favoured house slave learnt of it at the last moment and chose to betray the secret to his Master. When the band of black rebels, armed with cutlasses and scythes, slipped out of the slave lines late in the evening to attack the Great House, they found the white men waiting for them in ambush.

The rebels were shot down like wild hogs in their frantic scramble up the slope of the hill. Before he died, one of them brought the blade of his cutlass down upon the neck of a young overseer; the rest fell in the dust and cane trash which littered the cobbled apron outside the factory. Their blood ran into the gutter which carried the rain water to the horse troughs at the bottom of the hill. The slaves who were killed outright were soon seen to have been the lucky ones; for the wounded survivors, chained in the cellars beneath the factory, the planters' code of that time prescribed a more elaborate death.

At sunrise next morning, young James Langford saw a company of the Militia arrive from Bridgetown in their stained green tunics. The women and children of the slave lines were turned out of their huts to watch, the children deliberately placed in the front rank so that the lesson should not be lost on them.

The six rebels who still lived were carried out of the cellars and pinned with forked sticks to the earth in front of their huts. The estate blacksmith, a slave himself, heated six iron rods to white heat in an open hearth set up for the purpose on the site. At a signal from the Master, he approached each rebel in turn and thrust the glowing point of one of the rods deep into the man's groin. Immediately afterwards, two of the smith's assistants heaped dry cane trash upon the writhing men; then they were burnt alive.

The fire was lit at their feet, and those who had not been seriously wounded in the ambush took a long time to die. Some cried out so loudly in their agony that the estate dogs whimpered in alarm; but James Langford, watching from a distance with the other white boys of the estate, witnessed the big Mandingo endure his fate without a sound. When at last he was dead, and before the fire consumed his body, young James approached the corpse and saw that the black man had bitten through his tongue in his extremity rather than beg the white Master for mercy.

At the far side of the field, a second white overseer watched Robert and his family with interest. The man raised his hand in brief salute; Robert returned the greeting, but not one of the toiling slaves looked up from the earth in front of him for fear of his pantalooned driver's cowhide whip.

The overseer rode towards them.

'You looking for work?' he asked Robert. 'I can give you a place here with the horses.'

'I have a Deed for land of my own,' Robert replied. 'I only work for myself.'

'You own any niggras?' the man inquired.

Robert shook his head. 'I can manage without to begin with.'

The overseer was not impressed. 'Brave words,' he remarked cynically. 'I have heard them before.' He turned his horse. 'When you discover you are mistaken,' he said, 'come back here and I will give you work.'

The family moved on.

'If our harvest this year in Grenada had been good,' Robert said to his wife when they had walked a little distance, 'there would have been money enough for us to buy a niggra. I would have gone to an auction in the capital and brought back a strong young buck. Next year perhaps we could have bought a female and then we could have bred them. I had thought about it often . . .'

His wife searched for words to soothe the hurt.

'We will start again on our new land,' she said. 'It will be easier the second time because we have experience now. It will not be long before we have money again . . .'

But Robert could not share his wife's faith that all would be well once more. It seemed to him that they had had their chance; and at the very moment of success God had seen fit to level them in the dust.

On the back of the mule, the younger boy began to cry softly because of the rawness between his legs. They stopped in the shade of a stand of tall bamboo and Robert lifted both children to the ground. They ate a little of the dry bread they had bought in the market place on the waterfront and stretched themselves out to rest upon the carpet of fallen bamboo leaves. A pair of golden heliconid butterflies settled

22

on the broad hindquarters of the sweating mule.

Not long after they resumed their journey, they found that the road they followed passed amongst a scattered collection of palm-thatched huts. The villagers were all mulattoes who, by one means or another, had contrived to purchase their freedom. The men were smiths and carpenters and a few had boldly set up in business for themselves; because their skills were needed, they were hired from time to time by the white planters of the area. It was an uneasy relationship and the planters looked without pleasure at the situation in some of the neighbouring West Indian islands where free mulattoes were beginning to exert an unwelcome influence on the conduct of affairs.

The mulatto women greeted Robert and his family as they passed by. There had been few mulattoes in Grenada and none at all where he had worked on the Honduran coast, and Robert was struck by the long-legged grace and the fine, patrician features of the coloured girls.

From one of the women he bought a few oranges and three avocado pears, but no one there seemed to have heard of the place called Treasure Bay and from this Robert deduced that they still had many miles to walk. The children of the village were clearly puzzled by the presence of the family amongst them. The only white people they were used to seeing were the overseers in the fields of the estate and members of Ole Massa's family from the Great House, who occasionally passed that way on horseback. The sight of white peasants who were clearly no better off than their own families was an event for which they had not been prepared, and they stared with round-eyed fascination until reminded of their manners by the flat of their mothers' hands.

On the morning of the fourth day, the family arrived at a fork in the road and took the track which led south towards the sea. The fields of sugar cane gave place after a while to open, uncultivated savannah and then, without warning, they reached the place Robert had noted on the map in the Land Office where the track crossed the river.

The river was broad and swift-flowing and, as Robert had suspected, there was no sign of either bridge or ferry. Fortunately, it had not rained heavily in the mountains for several weeks and the water was not deep. They waded warily across, hauling the unhappy mule behind them, with Robert watching out for the presence of crocodiles which they had been warned were common all along the southern plain.

In the late afternoon they reached their land. It proved to be as flat and featureless as the clerk had described it. Where it was bounded by the sea, there was a fine expanse of coral sand which pleased them; but had they been able to view the place from the air, like the scissor-tailed frigate birds which rode the wind currents high above them, they would have seen that the beach was only a short interval in an otherwise unbroken coastline of stilt-legged mangroves and broad mud flats.

'We must give a name to the place,' Agatha said. 'What shall we call it?'

Robert shrugged his shoulders. 'Call it what you please,' he replied.

'Then I name it New Hope,' she said, 'because that is what it offers us.'

About a mile to the east, the river they had crossed earlier in the day flowed quietly into the sea; but as they soon discovered, when the rains came the river overtopped its low banks and, without ditches or drains, large areas of the surrounding land were flooded. Near the river, the face of the savannah was studded with evil-smelling stagnant pools which never completely dried up even in the most severe drought. The opaque, green water bred ferocious armies of mosquitoes and, at dusk, the evening light was dimmed by their numbers as if a black lace curtain had been drawn across the sky.

On the first night of their arrival, they were forced to sleep beside a green wood fire in a futile attempt to escape the insects and, next morning, they found it hard to say whether the effects of the thick grey smoke had been more or less aggravating then the attentions of the mosquitoes themselves.

On the following day, Robert selected an elevated circle of land on which to raise the family hut and they capped the mud and wattle walls with a conical roof of plaited coconut boughs. One of the boys discovered on the beach an oak-staved hogshead which had fallen from the deck of some passing vessel, and they used it to collect rainwater trapped in the bamboo guttering which Robert hung beneath the eaves of the hut.

The next priority was to lay out a provision ground beside their hut so that they should not starve. It was light work to clear the thin cloak of thorn and scrub from the soil to plant yam and sweet potato and long-eared maize; but almost at once Robert noted unhappily as he used his spade that the water table lay only a few inches beneath the surface of the soil. As the first weak shoots pushed reluctantly up through the earth, he confided to Agatha: 'The soil is too wet. If it will not support good maize, then the cane we grow will prove worthless.'

But she would not give way to his pessimism.

'In that case we must do the best with what we have,' she replied simply. 'God spared us to escape the French and there are many worse off than we. We must thank Him for what He has done for us and expect no more than He chooses to give.'

Robert's belief in a God who really cared for him, however, had not survived the loss of his land in Grenada.

'I expect nothing and in future I shall ask for nothing,' he said bitterly.

The nearest village to their land was seven miles away; the track which led to it was rough at the best of times and became impassable as soon as the rains arrived in March each year. Because of this, the family were obliged to make themselves entirely self-sufficient. There were fish in the sea that bordered their land, and the shallow eel grass beds offshore supported a population of giant queen conches and helmet shells which they roasted in their porcelain jackets over a driftwood fire on the beach. At certain seasons, they ate the bright yellow roe of the white sea urchins which grazed the eel grass flats and, from time to time, they made a kind of jellied pudding from the fronds of a succulent sea weed which grew in the deeper water beyond the eel grass. Occasionally, it proved possible to trap an incautious female turtle as she struggled ashore when the moon was full to lay her eggs in the dry sand at the upper margin of the beach; and, when all else failed, there were the nocturnal, red-backed land crabs that lived deep in the twisting burrows which honeycombed the banks of the river. But the yams and sweet potatoes, on which they had relied to fill their bellies during the early years in Grenada, were so bloated and bitter here that they could scarcely be eaten at all.

The diet on which they lived proved sufficient to keep them alive, but it robbed them of their strength and energy, and it seemed to Robert and Agatha that the two growing boys were perpetually hungry. Even the raw-boned mule grew frail and listless on the poor scrub around the hut which was all that it could find.

On those days when the south-east trades were supplanted by fiercer winds from the west which whipped up the surface of the sea and prevented them from fishing, the two boys, William and Thomas, would cross the open scrubland to the stands of red mangrove that lined both banks of the river. Flocks of steel-blue gaulins perched among the branches and the boys climbed the swaying root buttresses to steal the eggs from the birds' untidy nests. They ate the eggs raw, sitting side by side within the cool, green chamber at the heart of the mangroves with the arched branches meeting in a high Gothic ceiling above their heads.

The brown river itself was full of crocodile, and sometimes in the late evening herds of ponderous manatee made their way in from the sea to browse on the water plants anchored in the soft mud of the river floor. The manatee, for all their bulk, were shy, inoffensive creatures that threatened no one; but there was an occasion, not long after their arrival at Treasure Bay, when the two boys carelessly crossed the path of a female crocodile. The creature was in the act of ferrying her young in her jaws from the place where they had hatched to the security of the water.

Without an instant's hesitation, the crocodile jettisoned her offspring and charged the boys, her jaws held wide in fury, her broad tail flattening the mangrove saplings all about her. The boys leapt for safety high into the nearest mangrove and, eventually, the crocodile grew weary of waiting for them to come down and departed to collect her scattered brood.

Agatha and the boys helped Robert with the task of clearing the thin covering of scrub from the rectangle of land which he paced out behind their hut and which he intended as their first field of cane. Together they planted the chosen place with cuttings and, when these had taken root in the soil, they discovered that the job of weeding between the rows, which had demanded so much effort in Grenada, proved light work here because there was no swift resurgence of weeds once the land had been cleared.

The boys remarked on this fact with pleasure and surprise, but Robert knew that it only confirmed what he had feared most: the land was too wet and too salt, much as it had been in Honduras along the narrow belt between the sea and the rain forest where he had felled his logs.

He said to the boys: 'We must not expect much from this soil. If the weeds do not care for it, neither will the cane. The land needs to be drained; only then will the rain have a chance to wash the salt out of the earth and make it fertile.'

But he knew that the task was well beyond the strength of himself and his family. A dozen slaves could do it in a month, with a diligent overseer to encourage them with his whip; but he possessed no slaves and lacked the money to hire any labour.

There were few trees on their land, but it was necessary to fell two giant silk cottons since the cane would not grow in their shade. They owned no saws, so the work had to be done with an axe. The sunken roots they destroyed with fire, heaping glowing charcoal embers all around them until the sap had been driven out and they would burn readily; then they extracted the charred remains from the earth like rotten teeth. Afterwards, they filled in the fire-stained cavities with soil carried from the river bank.

Robert knew that the slaves who came from the Guinea Coast believed that the bole of every silk cotton tree harboured a malign spirit which they called a *moko-jumbie*, and which was known to inflict a cruel vengeance upon any human being rash enough to disturb it. It was a belief so strongly held that even some superstitious white peasants had come to share it; but, when he looked, Robert found that the hollow boles of the giant trees contained only a terrified family of manicous and the nests of half a dozen white owls. He despatched with the handle of his axe one of the female manicous and Agatha roasted the unappetising rodent over an open charcoal fire for their evening meal.

They cleared and planted with cane as much land as they could manage in those first months of their occupation; but the harvest the following year proved that Robert had been right: the cane was of the poorest quality, thin-stemmed, dry and without sweetness. Its value scarcely met the cost of hiring a bullock cart to transport it to the nearest sugar factory on a property several miles to the east.

The small reserve of silver coins – which Robert had cached in a hole dug out of the mud floor of their hut –

dwindled month by month in spite of every saving he could make. At the beginning of their third year at Treasure Bay there were only three coins left, and with these it was necessary to buy clothing for the boys since the rags they wore no longer covered their nakedness. Even the fat logger-head turtles, on which they had once relied for meat and for their soft-skinned eggs, seemed to visit the beach on increasingly rare occasions as some primeval instinct warned successive generations that the place had become unhealthy for them.

And so the fortunes of the Langford family on Saint Cecilia declined with each passing year. For Robert, caught up on a treadmill of endless labour to keep his family one step ahead of starvation, the future appeared to hold nothing but pain. There no longer seemed the smallest prospect of improving their miserable condition. The early years of struggle in Grenada, followed by the loss of everything he had worked for, had served to sap both the strength of his arms and his stubborn determination to succeed; and as they all grew physically weaker, so they became increasingly susceptible to the diseases of the island.

On Christmas Day 1785, Thomas, the younger boy, died of malaria. They could not bury him on their own land, because the water table lay too close to the surface, so Robert and William were obliged to carry the emaciated body to higher ground more than a mile away from their hut. They had nothing with which to fashion a coffin, so they laid the body naked in the earth and Agatha raised a little cairn of stones above it to mark the place.

When they had finished, Robert sent Agatha and William back to the hut ahead of him. It was evening and the sun fell beneath the taut arc of the horizon as he watched them go. Above the western sea, thin streamers of scarlet cloud were drawn out and then cut loose by the tide of the wind. He sat alone on the hard, sun-warmed earth by the grave of his son and he thought of his grandfather Cleydon. Cleydon had survived ten years of merciless labour on that hated Barbadian estate and his spirit had not been broken, but Robert could draw no strength for himself from the example of his grandfather's fortitude. Old Cleydon had never held success in the palm of his hand only to see it suddenly dashed away.

Robert returned to the family hut long after the blue-black tropical night had come down all in one piece like a shutter, but he brought no words of comfort for his wife or for his surviving son. After that day, a mood of hopeless despair settled upon the family as they clung without hope to their waterlogged, infertile land, and they grew silent and sullen among themselves in the cane field and in the evenings after dark.

2

The hurricane which struck the south coast of Saint Cecilia in September 1795 was preceded by a strange, unnatural stillness. The family had been working in their field of cane since sunrise. There had been a brief early shower of rain and so at first they had been glad of the heat of the sun. Their ragged clothes dried quickly on their backs. But as the morning grew older, what had at first been a healing warmth became more like the insufferable breath of a furnace. The comfort of what little wind drifted in from the sea was denied them by the green walls of cane which enclosed them in narrow, vaulted tunnels open at the top to the cloudless sky. The sweat ran off their bodies and fell upon the baked skin of the earth; the cruel, razor-sharp edges of the cane leaves drew blood on their exposed forearms and the salt sweat, draining into these shallow wounds, itched and stung unmercifully. The cane was almost fit for harvest, each pallid stem topped by a golden arrowhead of seed. To the family, grasping their hoes in the stifling heat, the silk tassled arrowheads seemed to twist and quiver in the diamond light.

In the middle of the morning they laid down their hoes and returned to the hut to take water. Immediately they sensed from the behaviour of the birds that something unusual was about to happen. The flocks of gaulins, which were accustomed to spend each day feeding in the shallow pockets of water near the river, had abandoned their hunting grounds and returned to their roosts in the mangroves. The air grew increasingly humid and oppressive; it seemed to bear down on Robert's shoulders with a persistent, tangible pressure. Every movement required a conscious effort of will.

An ominous silence hung over the land. The sea stretched away to the southern horizon like a sheet of beaten lead; only the occasional leap of a predatory houndfish disturbed the oily sheen upon the surface of the water.

A little before midday there was a curious, threatening convergence of cloud over the sea. Not long afterwards, a succession of steep-backed waves was driven in from the south, surged over the protective ellipse of the coral reef that ran parallel to the beach and broke heavily upon the sand. The wall of cloud rose into the sky until it obscured the sun; the family moved into the uncertain shelter of their hut in a twilight of pale, luminous grey.

As the mass of cloud closed the island, an opaque curtain of rain fell from beneath it and was swept towards them across the sea. The inverted V-shaped roof of the hut was beaten flat by a sudden cataract of water. The family huddled together in one corner of the hut, seeking what shelter they could find beneath a tar-stained sheet of canvas.

From the direction of the sea they could hear the approaching fury of the wind. It came first in a series of violent gusts. Robert peered out through one of the cracks in the rattan shutter which had been drawn across the window; he knew at once that they were to be spared nothing. At a point about a mile from the shore the natural division between the sea and the air above it had ceased to exist. He saw that the surface of the water had been beaten into a wild, convulsive wall of spume that was racing directly towards them.

The frail wattle hut collapsed without resistance. The broken roof went first, sailing into the air like an untethered kite; then the walls of mud and sticks disintegrated all about them. The canvas sheet was torn from their grasp; they were instantly exposed to the full fury of the storm. The wind howled about them, tearing at their hair, driving the raindrops into their eyes.

On the only point of higher ground, some two hundred yards from the site of their hut, there was a circle of granite boulders. Long ago the children had christened the place 'The Giants' Hearth' because of its shape. Now, pointing in the direction of the boulders, Robert yelled above the fury of the wind: 'We must shelter in the hearth before the river swells and bursts its banks.'

Grasping each other by the hand so that they should not be blown flat, they raced across the open ground, propelled by the wind behind them and lashed by the stinging rain. In the cramped space in the centre of the stone circle, the family cowered white-faced with cold and fear while the full force of the hurricane howled and gibbered above their heads.

The eye of the storm swept over them at midday, and it brought a sudden interlude of calm as frightening in its eerie, unexpected silence as the tumult of the hurricane itself. They waited helpless in the shelter of the rocks for the fury to descend upon them once again; it would come this time, they knew, from the opposite direction. When it returned, however, although the rain had not diminished, they found that the fortuitous position of the boulders gave them some protection from the wind. They lay huddled together like animals in their sodden, ragged clothes.

The hurricane passed on late that afternoon. When Robert and his son stood up to look over the top of the boulders, they saw that all around them the undrained land was under water. They were marooned as surely as if they had been cast upon a desert island. Of the mud and wattle hut which had provided them with shelter for eleven long years, and which had contained everything they owned, there was not the smallest trace. A torrent of pale brown water raced over the site, sweeping away the little mound on which the hut had stood, re-moulding the contours of the land over which it passed.

They had owned little; now they were left with nothing but the rags in which they were dressed. Surrounded by the flood, they were suddenly parched with thirst. One by one, they removed their sodden clothing and squeezed the water from it into their mouths. They did not speak; there was nothing left to say.

The flood receded during the course of the night. In the morning they collected branches stranded by the water and laid them over the circle of boulders to form a roof, so they were shielded at least from the fierce heat of the sun which reappeared in the wake of the storm as if the previous day had never been. By good fortune, the storm had thrown ashore an abundance of fish and they ate some of the fish raw because they had nothing with which to build a fire.

It was understood without discussion that now they would have to abandon their land. It had always been poor, infertile land but it had been their own and Robert had been his own master. Now he said, so softly that Agatha and the boy scarcely caught the words: 'I must find a Master to work for. It is what I should have done from the beginning when we knew the soil was salt. That overseer was right: we needed slaves to drain the land.'

'You did everything that any man could do,' Agatha replied. 'It is God's will and we must have faith in His justice.'

But her husband was not consoled.

'There is no God,' he said bitterly. 'And in this world there is no justice either.'

When the afternoon came, William left his parents in the shelter of the ring of boulders and wandered aimlessly across the land that they had cultivated. All the stands of cane had been uprooted and carried away by the first swift rush of water; the fields were buried now beneath a cloak of dun-coloured mud which steamed sullenly in the heat of the sun.

He walked down to the beach. The still-disturbed sea was stained by the torrent of water which poured from the mouth

34

of the river nearby; the familiar contours of the beach had been altered beyond all recognition by the fury of the waves which had assaulted it.

Where there had been a low rampart of sand raised above the level of the land behind it, there was now a broad depression. As William looked with tired, indifferent eyes at the transformation that had taken place, something on the sand less than a yard from where he stood caught the light of the sun. He knelt down and saw at once that it was an ill-shaped silver coin, not worn with use but as bright and fresh as on the day it had come from the mint. Beyond it there was another and another, all leading towards a hole in the disturbed sand from the mouth of which the sunlight was reflected by a thousand separate coins.

He tore off his ragged, sweat-stained shirt and filled it with the coins, and when it could hold no more, he thrust his hand deep into the hole. For as far down as he could reach, he could feel only the cold, silken touch of the coins. He raced back across the treacherous, slippery ground to the shelter among the boulders. Without a word he poured the contents of his shirt on to the wet floor in a river of shining silver, until the coins spilled over the feet of his parents. Then he returned to the beach to recover the rest of the treasure before the rising tide sealed up the entrance of the hole for ever.

It took William four separate journeys to the beach before the last coin was taken up from the sand; and within the circle of boulders the three of them sat silently in their discomfort staring with disbelief at the great pile of silver that carpeted the muddy floor.

In a voice that quivered with excitement and with a new found quality of hope, William said: 'There is no need for us to give up the land now. We can hire men to help us drain the soil. When the water table falls and the salt is washed away, the cane will grow tall and strong. Then we shall be able to buy slaves to work our land.'

He looked around him over the top of the boulders at the broad savannah still cloaked in its blanket of steaming mud, and in his mind's eye he saw the whole plain green with sugar cane from the margin of the sea to the distant foothills of the mountain range.

'We shall be a family of . . . substance,' he said, relishing the sound of the unfamiliar word.

His mother bowed her head and, with her son, thanked God for His favour.

Only Robert was silent, disapproving, unmoved by his son's bright vision of their future.

'Are you not happy that our fortune has changed?' Agatha asked him. 'Do you not think it is right that we should thank God for His mercy?'

Robert looked down at the silver coins piled about his feet.

'It has come too late for me,' he said in a voice so low that they could hardly hear it. 'The truth is that I no longer care about the land.'

3

There was never any mystery about the origin of the coins that William Langford found; their mint marks showed that they once formed part of the treasure captured by Henry Morgan when he took Panama City in 1670.

Morgan had sailed from Jamaica with only twelve hundred men, reduced the Spanish fort at San Lorenzo and then marched across the width of the isthmus. The Spanish garrison fled at his approach, setting fire to the city as they went. The treasure recovered from the ruins was shared out among all who took part in the adventure, according to rank. It is recorded that the most junior seaman received about four hundred of the silver pieces.

The cache that William found was most likely the share of a petty officer. The original owner of the coins had no doubt buried them on the beach for safe-keeping and for some reason he had failed to return to recover them at a later time. That unknown sailor could not have been the only man to have made use of the deserted beach for the purpose; it was by no accident that the place was given the name Treasure Bay by English settlers at the end of the seventeenth century.

Whatever the history of the money, there can be no uncertainty about its effect on the fortunes of the Langford family. Although the actual value of the cache proved to be modest when it was sold in the capital, it was enough. At one stroke, it gave them the means to drain their land and to raise dykes against the flooding of the river; just as William had foreseen, as soon as the water table was lowered and the rain had been given a chance to wash the salt from the soil, the land blossomed with cane whose sweetness and rich quality soon became a byword among the planters and sugar merchants of the island.

For Robert Langford, however, it had come too late; he never lived to see the rise of his family. Weakened by malaria, his spirit irreparably broken by the years of fruitless effort, he died less than a month after the hurricane had uncovered the cache of coins and made possible, at last, everything that he had wished to do.

He was sixty-one years old and they buried him beside his younger son on the higher ground that overlooked the sea.

The money brought an abrupt change in the way of life of William Langford and his mother. To drain their land, William hired a gang of free mulattoes from a village to the east of the river; and when that job was done, he employed the same men to build a modest clapboard house for Agatha and himself. He designed the building with five rooms and a broad verandah on which he and his mother slept during the hottest months of the year. Afterwards, he kept on six of the hired men to tend his cane fields. Hired labour was expensive and unreliable, but for the time being there was no other way.

For the first two years, he refused to assign any of the hired mulattoes to help his mother in the house; their labour was too precious on the land, where he drove them as hard as he dared to plant a larger and larger area with cane. When the product of the first harvest had been sold, however, and payment was demanded, and received, in gold coin, he decided that the time had arrived when he could dispense with the hired men and become an owner of slaves. And because he was a man who believed that time should not be wasted once a decision had been made, he set out on horseback for the capital at dawn next day.

The slave auction was held in an open square of ground on the waterfront not far from the place where the family had first come ashore on that distant, sweltering afternoon in 1779. William was only seven years old at the time, but he could still remember how the unfamiliar earth of Saint Cecilia had pitched and rolled beneath his feet after seven days aboard the Dutch ketch which had carried them from Grenada and the attentions of the French soldiers.

The open square was partially shaded by the spreading branches of a giant saman tree. The tree's reptilian roots coiled and writhed over the barren surface of the soil before plunging down into the heart of the island. A group of white planters was sitting together on benches, their backs propped against one of the largest roots which sprang like a buttress from the great bole of the trunk. A rough wooden platform had been set up on trestles in the centre of the square and the auctioneer had perched himself in a kind of pulpit beside the platform. The man was dressed in a long, grey coat and stained white pantaloons; he wore a tall, black hat and he reminded William of one of those predatory herons which stalked the river bank at the eastern border of his land. Behind the auctioneer, ranged along one side of the square, a small crowd of loafers, mostly sailors from the ships in port, looked on with a bored, indifferent curiosity.

The Africans offered for sale had arrived the previous day. The ship which brought them had been obliged to anchor in the roads beyond the mouth of the harbour, but even with this precaution taken the animal stink which rose from the open holds was caught by the inconstant wind and carried ashore. Several of the better dressed planters held lavender scented kerchiefs to their noses against the stench.

The Africans had been marshalled in two groups, men on one side of the platform, women and children on the other. Some of the more robust men had been manacled and the auctioneer had taken care to post guards from the ship to stand over them with muskets. During their short stay in Jamaica the previous week, two male slaves had contrived to escape while waiting for the auction to begin and, though they were soon recaptured, it had been necessary to hang them in the presence of the others to serve as a warning. Their deaths had meant to the auctioneer a net loss of several hundred guineas and he did not intend to allow the same thing to happen again.

The slaves squatted in the dust, swaying slightly on their haunches with the involuntary motion acquired after thirteen weeks of close confinement on the rolling, plunging vessel which had brought them from Africa across the Middle Passage. They did not speak to each other and they kept their gaze fixed firmly on the bare earth in front of them. From time to time, one of them relieved himself in the dust; a thick cloud of flies hovered over the two groups of apathetic men and women and gathered at the moist corners of their children's eyes.

William Langford took his place among the group of planters in the shade of the saman tree. The auctioneer's high pitched voice carried clearly across the square from his pulpit beside the platform.

'Now, gentlemen,' the man was saying as William settled himself at the end of a crowded bench, 'it is my pleasure to offer number seven, a fine Mandingo buck. As you good gentlemen will surely know, Mandingoes are the sweetest natured, most obedient niggers the dark continent has to offer – and strong, too. You will find no better specimen of the breed than this one I present to you.'

He motioned to one of his assistants to lead the slave to the centre of the wooden platform. The wretched African looked starved and ill; there were blue-black scars about his wrists where the manacles had bitten deep into the flesh. He stumbled on the boards and nearly fell.

'Just finding his land legs again, gentlemen,' the auctioneer countered smoothly. 'Now who will open with three hundred guineas?'

There was a brief, derisory laugh from the gathering of planters, followed by a long, impatient silence. At last, one planter sitting close to William shuffled his feet in the dust and spat ostentatiously. 'I will give you a hundred and twenty for the sickly brute,' he volunteered; and so the bidding got under way.

When the Mandingo had been sold, the rest of the slaves were led one at a time to the centre of the platform as the auctioneer called extravagant attention to their virtues. All the slaves were naked and the planters left their seats in the shade from time to time and climbed up to examine them with the same suspicious care they exercised when buying their horses. They pulled open the Africans' mouths to inspect their teeth, ran their hands over their bellies to check for incipient hernias and spread their buttocks to see whether they might be suffering from piles. The small crowd of hangers-on proffered their own coarse advice as the female slaves were handled in their turn.

The auctioneer maintained a spurious running patter about the merits of his goods, heaping superlatives upon them whenever the bidding faltered. But for all the man's practised eloquence, it was clear to everyone present that this was an indifferent lot of slaves. The cream of the shipment had been sold in Jamaica the previous week and nothing could disguise the fact that what had been brought on to Saint Cecilia was largely rejected stock. All the slaves bore the debilitating marks of their long imprisonment, first in the stockades of the Guinea Coast and later under hatches during the fearful journey across the Middle Passage. Those who were not physically ill seemed to have lost the will to live since being torn from their African villages.

The auctioneer, who was due to return immediately with his ship to the Guinea Coast to collect another cargo of Africans, knew that he must dispose of all his stock that day. There would be no profit in taking any of the slaves back to the ship with him. But the sale proceeded slowly and, after each unsatisfactory bid, the auctioneer fell into the habit of appealing loudly to God to witness that he was being ruined by the parsimonious planters of Saint Cecilia.

The slaves themselves seemed indifferent now to the matter of their disposal. Their faces were devoid of all expression as they were led in turn on to the platform where their futures were decided for them by the group of red-faced men who sat in the shade beneath the branches of the saman tree. Only once was there an incident to show that they, too, had human feelings: a single, high-pitched cry from a young mother whose eight-year-old son was taken from her and sold separately to a middle-aged planter with soft hands and rouged cheeks, who stroked the boy's slim buttocks before lifting him off the platform.

William watched impassively as the boy looked towards his mother and held out his hands in a gesture of silent farewell; then his new owner, irritated by the display, bundled him roughly into the carriage and drove off along the waterfront in a fine cloud of brick red dust.

William returned to New Hope three days later with seven slaves of his own. He had held his bid until close to the end of the auction when prices had reached as low as they were likely to get, so the quality of his new chattels was not high and one of the two female Africans was already close to the end of her breeding years. He did not mind, however, because she had been cheap to buy and one breeding female would be enough to begin with; concerning the males, he had no doubt that a well used cattle whip could squeeze as much work from a weaker man as from any young buck in his prime.

The slaves' first task was to build their own lines and then to plant a provision ground adjacent to it.

'You niggras will eat only what you grow for yourselves and what you can take from the sea when I give you time to fish there,' William told them on that first morning back at New Hope. 'Some Masters spoil their niggras with salt pork and corn meal so they grow fat and idle; you will learn I do not make that mistake.'

With the point of a sharpened stick, he laid out in the dust of the savannah precisely where they were to raise their huts and where they should site their pit latrine, well down wind from his own house. With the help of the same stick, he divided the area of the provision ground into seven equal sized plots, allocating one plot to each man and woman by name.

The slaves understood no more than a few English phrases, but they did not miss the purport of their Master's words. Within the space of a month, the red earth of the provision ground was mottled with green shoots of yam and manioc and sweet potato; and William saw to it that on Sundays, when every slave by law was excused work in the cane fields, they laboured from dawn to sunset on their provision ground. Sickly, undernourished niggras, as he informed his mother, were a poor return on the money that had bought them.

During his father's lifetime, William Langford had been given little opportunity to display his own initiative. He was small boned and narrow chested and he had been over-shadowed by both his father's strong personality and his large physical presence. His father had never chosen to regard him as an equal. Once freed from the constraint of Robert's pessimistic, overbearing nature, however, it soon became apparent that William's laconic, withdrawn manner con-cealed an innate talent for making money. He was methodi-cal, cunning and utterly determined to succeed; and his single-minded strength of purpose quickly served to earn him a reputation as a ruthless slave-master.

William did not regard Africans as human beings in the same sense as people with white skins. 'They are fashioned as beasts of burden,' he used to say to his mother whenever even she felt compelled to chide him for his harshness towards them. 'They are like mules: they respect only the lash.'

43

And to impress upon his unfortunate slaves that they were no more than his personal goods, to dispose of as he chose, he branded them like mules with the initial letter of his surname neatly contained in a broad ellipse. It would have been possible for him to arrange that the branding should be carried out by a blacksmith hired for the purpose from another property, but William Langford chose to do the job himself. He branded the men on the shoulder just beneath the shadow of the collar bone and the women upon the left breast, two finger's breadth above the nipple.

The property of New Hope flourished in the years which followed that first purchase of slaves. On the distant European market the price of raw sugar continued steadily to rise and, after each cane harvest, William made use of his profits to acquire more land and more slaves. He was obliged to pay the Government for the land now, but in the area of Treasure Bay it remained cheap because few planters were prepared ·to meet the expense of draining it before they could plant their first crops. The fact that the land, once drained, proved more fertile and productive even than the coveted river valleys with their fine alluvial soil was a secret which William shrewdly kept to himself.

'People are fools,' he confided to his mother. 'Because we still choose to live in a clapboard house and wear osnaburg clothes they believe we remain paupers. Well, let them think so.'

By 1807, New Hope encompassed more than two hundred acres and William Langford was the registered owner of fifty-three adult slaves and nineteen slave children. Six years later there were one hundred and seven slaves and the northern boundary of the estate had been pushed back two and a half miles from the sea. In that same year, William hired his first white overseer and, immediately after the next cane harvest, he determined to build his own sugar factory. Up to that time he had been obliged to sell his harvested cane to one of the larger estates in that part of the island which possessed a factory, and he had found increasingly hard to bear the thought that other men were making a handsome profit from what he always saw as an unequal arrangement.

He sited his own factory astride the spur of one of the few outcrops of high ground that occurred on his land, in order to take advantage of the force of gravity in the intricate process that produced raw sugar from green lengths of cane stalk. Using the labour of his slaves, and with the occasional advice of an engineer from another property for whose services he was reluctantly obliged to pay, the factory was completed in seven months, in good time to process the next harvest of cane.

It was built of rectangular blocks of white limestone which had been carved out of the ground with axes and long, two-handled saws. At the highest level William set the mill house, to the mouth of which led all roads from the cane fields. The cane arrived on the backs of donkeys and the animals were unloaded on the paved apron in front of the mill house and returned at once to the fields. Inside, a gang of slaves fed the cane into a pair of hard wood rollers which were turned by yoked oxen. A party of female slaves was stationed on the far side of the rollers and collected the crushed pulp as it passed out. They carried it away to be employed a second time as fuel to stoke the boiler fires.

The juice from the cane stalks fell into a tray beneath the rollers; it was drained away by an underground pipe to a collecting cistern in the boiling house, which occupied the second level of the factory. From the cistern the juice was led into the first of five large coppers where it was boiled. A ring of slaves armed with wooden ladles stood around each of the coppers and removed the thick scum which rose to the surface. The juice was ladled from one copper to another until it reached the fifth and last, when it was ready for crystallisation. It was hot, skilled and back-breaking labour,

45

and William made a point of posting his two fiercest Negro drivers to stand behind the slaves who worked in the boiling house: lazy work here could result in second quality sugar which fetched a lower price, and that possibility was enough to keep William Langford awake in his bed and the unfortunate slaves cringing under their drivers' whips.

Over the last of the five boiling coppers he posted the most skilled slave of all. The man waited there until his experience told him that the bubbling, viscous liquid had reached the critical stage; then, at his signal, another gang of sweating slaves transferred it to the cooling tank where the shining sugar crystals formed.

As the rich brown liquid cooled, it was ladled into tapering wooden pots and carried to the filling room where it lay undisturbed for two days. On the third day, at William's order, the pots were removed to the curing house and the crystals of sugar separated from the viscous molasses. A month after the wooden pots had been taken down to the curing house they were heaved on their sides, the contents knocked out of them and the heavy brown sugar raked into glistening pyramids upon the floor.

William's mother, Agatha, did not live to see the factory completed. She died in 1812, carried off by an epidemic of cholera that also took three of the house slaves and several black children. William buried her next to her husband, raising above the two graves a single modest headstone fashioned from one of the rejected white limestone blocks which were being used to build his factory. He was too caught up in the work to find time to grieve unduly for his mother; during the last months of her life he had been vexed with her because she thought him unwise to build the factory until he had accumulated more money, and she told him so. Though he had tried to hide the knowledge from her, she knew that the cost of the factory would consume every penny of his savings.

'You should keep something in hand against bad times,' she warned him. 'You can never tell what blows life may have in store for you. The price of sugar will not stay high for ever.'

But William had been too impatient to delay the work for another year; the thought of the additional profit that a factory would bring for once over-rode his prudent instincts, and he answered his mother with harsh words for her unwelcome interference.

Unlike the great majority of unmarried white planters, William Langford did not choose a concubine from among the younger of his female slaves. He felt no need of such recreation. His sole pleasure seemed to lie in the development of his property and the ceaseless pursuit of profit, but he never experienced that curious, almost mystical, attachment to the soil which his father had felt so strongly and which had been tragically destroyed for him by disasters that were not of his own making. William's bond with the land was devoid of emotion; for him it was a means to wealth, and the possession of wealth was an end complete in itself.

Once every four months he paid a visit to the capital for reasons of business, but he had no friends there and he never stayed in the place for one minute longer than was necessary. He was never tempted to divert a shilling of his money towards his own physical comfort and it never occurred to him to improve his wardrobe as his wealth increased. The clothes he wore on his visits to the capital were ill-fitting and of the coarsest material. The merchants and shipping agents with whom he did business joked openly about the manner in which he dressed. His reputation generally was that of a crude and miserly man, and on the verandahs of his colleagues' estate houses his uncouth habits became the stuff of countless after-dinner anecdotes, all ribald and derisory.

If William ever caught an echo of the laughter, however, it troubled him not at all, and when news got about that he had amassed enough money to build his own factory at New Hope, he remained quite indifferent to the swift concession by his detractors that, after all, he was a much smarter man than his appearance had suggested.

The blow that rocked the sugar planters of the West Indies at the end of the Napoleonic wars was the more devastating because it was so unexpected. The signs had been there all along, but people had not cared to recognise them. At least part of the blame, it was seen with the benefit of hindsight, lay with the vanquished Corsican tyrant who had introduced Europeans to the possibilities of beet sugar. By the beginning of 1816, the price of raw cane sugar from the Caribbean which, not long before, had risen as high as seventy shillings a hundredweight was now on an inexorable slide to the point where all profit margins evaporated, and creditors – in the manner of their kind – gathered like vultures around the hapless planters to call in their dues.

On Saint Cecilia, as on the other West Indian islands, it was the smaller estates that were the first to feel the weight of the blow; and New Hope, for all William's efforts, was still numbered among these. He found the sudden reverse more difficult to bear than most. Ever since his father's death, he had known only increasing success. Each year had proved more profitable than the one before. Now estates larger than his own were being forced into debt and, in some cases, abandoned by their desperate owners. It was a time when each planter needed the cushion of money put by in order to survive, and William had spent every shilling of his own savings to build his new factory. His mother had proved more far-sighted than her son, and the knowledge was a special agony to him. Every morning now, as he stepped from his bedroom on to the verandah of his mean little house, the sight of his factory perched on its spur of higher ground served only to reprove him for his reckless ambition.

The land that constituted the property of New Hope in 1816 was bounded to the east by the river and to the west by a morass in which a forest of mangroves eventually gave place to a flat and useless expanse of reeds and water lillies. To the south, of course, there was only the sea. Northwards, however, where the flat land of the savannah began to slope upwards towards the foothills of the central mountain range, the border was now drawn along a wavering line where New Hope met another, long established property known as Providence.

Providence estate was owned by Jonas Bartlett, a tall, cadaverous man with a wrinkled, yellow skin and the cast of sickness on his face. His property was larger than William's and had boasted its own sugar factory for more than fifty years. He had been one of those planters who, from time to time, had bought up William's harvest and crushed it along with his own crop of cane. Twice a year he shipped out his hogsheads of raw sugar by shallow draught lighter down the length of the river that bordered William's land. The same merchant schooners which had recently begun to dock alongside the jetty that William had constructed for them at New Hope also took away in their holds the produce of Providence – but at much greater cost to that estate, as William had several times reflected with some satisfaction.

As the weeks passed and the price of sugar on the European market continued its disastrous fall, William Langford searched the depths of his soul for some means of saving his property. The solution came to him in the night when he was asleep, or that was how he came to recollect the miracle in later years, because it was already formed and present in his mind when he woke at first light one fateful morning.

It had been plain to William from the beginning that only those owners who took the harshest and most determined measures to economise were going to survive the bad times that were upon them, and the idea which came to him as he slept was of a merger between the New Hope and Providence estates that would permit savings possible in no other way. He had no means of knowing for sure what kind of predicament his neighbour might be in, but he felt confident that Jonas, too, must be searching his mind for some means to hold on to what he owned.

William's plan was quite straightforward: as soon as the two estates became one, the older of the two sugar factories would be dismantled and the machinery sold off to the highest bidder, half the slave population of each property would be taken to auction, and every service that was duplicated would be scrapped at once. Neither property on its own could exist for long in the circumstances that prevailed; but together, there was an even chance that they could hold out until better times returned. Of one matter he was quite convinced: there was no other way out for him.

William's immediate and most difficult task was to persuade his neighbour to play his part in the grand design. Every evening for the next three weeks, William sat huddled in his decrepit rattan chair on the back verandah of his little dwelling and gazed north towards the foothills of the mountain range and the fields of Jonas Bartlett's property, turning the problem over and over in his mind. The chief obstacle was all too evident: Providence, by any reckoning, was a larger, more valuable property than New Hope, and Jonas Bartlett owned at least twice as many slaves as William did; yet William was not prepared to settle for less than an equal share of the joint property. Clearly it would be necessary for him to throw into the balance something else which was of value to his neighbour, but William owned nothing beyond what could be measured or counted on his land at New Hope.

Then, in much the same unexpected manner in which he had struck upon the original idea, the solution to this equally daunting problem occurred to him as he dozed uneasily one afternoon in his rattan chair. It was a Sunday and his sudden cry of triumph brought his personal slave racing from the kitchen where he, too, had been dozing, fearful that he had somehow managed to displease his Master; but William had no need of him.

Jonas Bartlett was ten years older than William Langford. He had been widowed many years earlier and his dead wife had left him to bring up their four-year-old daughter. In 1816, the girl was thirty-six years old, lank-haired, plain and without a trace of the feminine graces that a mother would have instilled in her. Her father had long given up hope that someone might one day marry her and that there would be a child to keep the estate in the Bartlett family.

William Langford's approach to Jonas Bartlett was characteristically direct. He mounted his horse that same Sunday afternoon and rode out across the common boundary of the two estates to Jonas's rambling, shingle-roofed Great House. He had dressed himself hurriedly in the same ill-fitting, travel-stained clothes he wore for his visits to the capital and he was armed with a carefully thought out proposition. If he, too, lacked any hint of the social graces, he was at least known for the habit of making himself clear on matters of business.

The boundary between the two properties was marked by a windbreak of galba trees, pierced at one point by a track that allowed passage to a man on horseback but was too narrow to admit an ox cart or a carriage. As he passed from his own land into that of his neighbour, William saw with satisfaction that the cane fields on the far side of the galba trees were noticeably less well maintained than his own. Their untidy condition suggested a need of supervision that he would never have tolerated at New Hope.

The bridle track ran between the slaves' provision ground and their quarters. Since it was Sunday, the men and women themselves were at work on their personal plots of land. On several estates in other parts of the island some misguided owners were now allowing the missionaries to preach to their slaves on Sundays, so that the black men and women spent a large part of that day sitting in Baptist chapels instead of cultivating their provision grounds. It was a development William abhorred; he was glad to know that in this matter, at least, Jonas Bartlett shared his views. There was no chapel at Providence, and the last missionary to visit the property had been seen off by a pack of watch dogs unleashed by Jonas himself. William had no doubt that it was the same interfering Baptist he had personally hustled off his own land less than a month before. They were persistent devils.

Not far from the slave lines Jonas had built the estate gaol, a squat stone building with a hinged iron grille which served as its door. The grille stood open showing that, for the moment, there were no slaves in detention. Fixed to one wall of the gaol, however, about seven feet from the ground, there were two metal rings. It was from these rings that insubordinate slaves were suspended by their wrists when it became necessary to have them flogged. William noted with approval that the rings were bright from regular use; rusting punishment rings were a sign of a weak-willed owner whose slaves were sure to lack discipline. At New Hope, the three pairs of rings which he had fixed to the wall of his new factory were rarely out of use for more than a few days at a time.

The track swung sharply to the left and then opened out on to the cobbled apron of Jonas Bartlett's sugar factory. Crop time was still several months away so the factory stood idle, the doors leading to the boiler room shut fast. The design of the factory was old-fashioned and inefficient, and the tall brick chimney was wrapped about in places by broad iron bands to hold its loosening bricks together. The area around the building was still littered with mouldering trash left over from the last cane harvest, and in a number of places the fabric of the building was in urgent need of repair. William took heart for his mission from these clear signs that Providence was not doing well.

Jonas Bartlett was sprawled in a tall wicker chair on his front verandah when William Langford rode up the driveway to his house. His boots were off and in one large hand he cradled a tumbler of white rum. The smoke from his stained clay pipe hung in an evil-smelling cloud above his balding head. He had spent most of the morning reluctantly examining the accounts of his estate and in those unwelcome figures he had found the first unmistakable signs of his impending ruin. With the help of the rum, he intended for a few more hours to ward off the leprous spectre of bankruptcy. He was not expecting visitors.

William dismounted and handed the reins of his horse to the black groom who came running from the stables. Without rising from his chair – for he had always regarded the parvenu William as a social inferior – Jonas Bartlett shouted down the front steps in irritated greeting: 'Well, Langford, what brings you to Providence this time on a Sunday afternoon? You should have sent a boy over to tell me you were coming; you find me unprepared for guests.' He struggled to lace his boots, and then, his hospitable instincts reasserting themselves, 'Come up anyway and tell me your news,' he said.

The two men were accustomed to visit each other once or twice a year, to discuss the current price of slaves and other related matters, and privately to assess how well the other might be doing. But in the past these visits had always come about in response to an invitation and, though they had a guarded respect for each other, they had never been close and neither had ever before called on the other uninvited.

William seated himself on the chair which Jonas pulled up to the table for him; his host yelled for a servant to bring a glass, a jug of water and another bottle of rum. When they arrived on a tray, Jonas filled the glass with the oily, colourless spirit and pushed it towards his guest.

'To better crops and breeding slaves,' he said, raising his own glass in the time honoured planters' ritual.

William nodded; he scarcely ever drank, but he knew the form well enough. 'To them both,' he replied, and both men drained their glasses.

'Well,' Jonas inquired, once the conventions had been observed, 'what brings you?'

'I have a proposition to put,' William replied without preamble.

Jonas unlaced his boots again.

'Then let us hear what it is, man,' he said; and William told him.

The proposal had about it the clean virtue of simplicity. While another man might have suffered embarrassment in stating it, William Langford felt none because it was no more than a business proposition. The terms were quite straight-forward: the estates of New Hope and Providence should be merged into a single property, each owner holding an equal share of the value, but with William appointed manager. In return, and to make up for the acknowledged disparity in the worth of the two properties, he would marry Jonas's daughter; the offspring of the marriage, in due time, would inherit it all.

By scrapping the older of the two factories, reducing the population of slaves and economising in every possible way, the joint property could be kept out of the hands of the money lenders until the market improved. Fused together, William announced – and he did not conceal that this was the true purpose of his plan – both estates could survive the crisis that assailed them; separately, they would both be lost. And, in the way of a bonus for each man, a child of the union would ensure that their land would not fall into the hands of strangers after they were dead.

In many respects, and in spite of his pretensions to a better social background, Jonas Bartlett was not unlike William Langford. The life of a sugar planter produced unsen-timental men of similar outlook. Jonas, too, had built up his estate from uncertain beginnings and could not bear to contemplate its loss, but he knew better than to reveal at once the fact that the proposition pleased him.

The two men haggled through the night; agreement was not reached until the early hours of the morning. The marriage would take place at once, then the two properties would be merged to form a single company, the old factory at Providence would be closed down and the machinery sold off, and one half of each man's slave population would be put up for auction in the capital within the month. William and his bride would live with Jonas in his larger house, each man would hold an equal share in the new venture, and William would be appointed manager as he demanded. Finally, a formal, binding Agreement would be drawn up by a lawyer in the capital setting out the terms so that there should be no room for future misunderstanding. The merged estates, claiming something from each name, would be known as New Providence.

Only after William had at last returned to his own property, weary but triumphant as the sun was rising over the land that was to become one estate, did Jonas Bartlett trouble to inform his daughter that she was to be married to their neighbour the following week and that she should not fail to produce a son within the year.

In the event, the terms of the formal Agreement drawn up between William Langford and Jonas Bartlett were carried through to the letter. New Providence survived the bad times, while larger and wealthier properties all over Saint Cecilia fell into the hands of their creditors and were broken up; and that most important thing took place which was greatly hoped for but could not be guaranteed: Jonas's daughter, Margaret, always obedient to her father's wishes, produced three children in quick succession. Although the first two did not long survive, the youngest child was a strapping, healthy boy who showed no inclination towards sickness of any kind. They christened him Jonas in honour of his grandfather, who died at peace at New Providence as soon as he had witnessed the birth of the grandson he had wished for.

The following year, the demand for West Indian sugar on the European market suddenly revived. The price, which in its headlong fall had carried down to ruin so many less resourceful planters, now rose to its previous level. Within six months it stood at a record figure. Immediately, the sugar plantations of Saint Cecilia began to prosper once again. The good times had returned.

So it was that out of that curious, cold-blooded compact between the two neighbours, like honey from the carcase of Samson's lion, came sweet things: a successful marriage, a large and well-founded property, and an heir to it all, son of one partner and grandson of the other.

It proved to be, in its own way, a triumph of common sense over the dead hand of convention, and none of the parties involved ever had reason to regret a single clause of it.

4

Young Jonas Langford grew up at New Providence far from the company of other children his own colour, and so it was natural that he should have sought his friends among the children of the free coloured overseers and his father's slaves.

Although he was treated by the black men and women of the slave lines with the quiet deference due to the Master's heir, among the children all distinctions tended to be forgotten in the excitement of the games they played together. Jonas learned to hold his own at running and climbing – and occasionally fighting – without the help of any advantage conferred upon him by his white skin. He accepted as a fact of life that at the end of the day he and his friends returned from their games to very different surroundings, but it never occurred to him to imagine that he was in any way superior because his house was bigger than theirs. He thought of the black children with whom he played very much as any other child thinks of his friends and equals; and he took it for granted, in his innocence, that they thought of him in the same way.

When Jonas was nine years old, however, an incident took place which he was to remember for the rest of his life. He was engaged one morning in a furious sword fight with a young slave child called Zacky, a tall, cheerful, powerfully built boy a year older than himself. Of all the boys he knew, Zacky was the one he regarded as his special friend. The two children pursued each other across the broad, sun-baked square in front of the slave lines, dodging behind the mango tree at the edge of the clearing, their guango wood swords clashing, their mock oaths and loud laughter ringing around the open space. When they had fought each other to a standstill, they dropped their swords and ran to the water butt which stood beneath the split bamboo guttering at one end of the file of wattle huts.

Jonas took a deep draught of the cool water and, with the calabash still raised to his lips, his face flushed with excitement, he announced: 'When I grow up, Zacky, I goin' to be a soldier.' And without pausing to consider, he inquired: 'What you goin' be, Zacky?'

There was a long moment of silence; then, in a quiet, matter of fact voice Zacky replied: 'I goin' be your slave, Massa Jonas,' and the boy ran his fingers lightly over the raised outline of the letter L which had been branded into the soft, blue-black skin beneath the collar bone when he was eight years old.

After that morning, it seemed to Jonas that much of the fun had vanished from the games he played with his friend Zacky and the other boys. In his mind, an invisible barrier had suddenly dropped into place between them. Whenever he won a race, from that time on, or he beat one of the boys in a wrestling match, the pleasure of victory was hopelessly tainted by the suspicion that they might have let him win because of who he was.

Jonas Langford was born at the beginning of a period of fierce social upheaval in the West Indian islands. Slavery had by then existed for close on three hundred years, and from its unjust horrors a small group of white men in Europe and the Caribbean had made huge fortunes for themselves; now, as more and more Englishmen found it impossible any longer to reconcile their Christian faith with a system that decreed one human being to be the chattel of another, the whole rotten institution came under furious attack.

In England, the Abolitionists pushed from the top and, in the islands, the slaves themselves, encouraged by the missionaries, pushed as best they could from the bottom; the slave owners on their plantations were caught uncomfortably in the middle. As the pressures grew stronger, they reacted by becoming more and more intransigent, and in their island legislatures they passed increasingly ferocious laws to keep their restless slaves in line.

William Langford, like every other planter on Saint Cecilia, was utterly opposed to Abolition; the very word had for him the smell of ruin and revolution about it, and he forbade its use at New Providence. There were men he knew who piously affected to base their opposition to freedom for the slaves upon various well-thumbed passages of the Old Testament and the subordinate role which God himself was supposed to have chosen for the descendants of Ham; and there were others who declared that it was in the very nature of things that the white man should command the black. But William cared nothing for arguments like these. He took a more pragmatic view.

'The niggras have got to remain slaves,' he declared simply, 'because if we had to pay them for their labour it would ruin us.'

The delicate, dangerous situation in the meantime was aggravated everywhere by the missionaries. From the pulpits of their Baptist and Wesleyan chapels, they encouraged the slaves to press harder for their freedom; and, inevitably, a bitter animosity grew up between those men of God and the embattled planters. And while the more aggressive slaves plotted together at night in their wattle huts, their owners transformed their own Great Houses into fortresses against a sudden rising, with musket slits carved through stone walls and iron bars fitted to ornate mahogany door frames.

A dark cloud of fear and mistrust settled ominously over the beautiful islands of the Caribbean, and Saint Cecilia was not excepted.

When Jonas was twelve years old, his father engaged a

59

young English curate to live at New Providence and to educate his son. William himself was barely literate and, as the affairs of his property grew increasingly complex, he felt severely the handicap of his lack of education. He was forced to entrust the keeping of his account books to other people, and the fear that one day he might be cheated by his book-keepers, and never know of it, often woke him from his sleep in the dead hours of the night. He was determined that his son should not suffer in the same way.

The clergyman, when he arrived fresh-faced from Bristol, turned out to be a sensible and perceptive young man, and he succeeded in opening his charge's mind to the realisation that there was a larger world beyond the coasts of Saint Cecilia and that there were things in life at least as important as making an annual profit from a crop of sugar cane.

'There are many white families on this island who have never learnt either of those truths,' he remarked to Jonas. 'And the quality of their lives reflects their ignorance.'

He did not add that chief among the people he had in mind were his employer and his wife, but this truth was already apparent to Jonas.

Jonas applied himself to his lessons; in due course he acquired a good general education. The account books of New Providence were never to cause him a moment's loss of sleep.

He grew up fair haired and broad in the shoulder like his great-grandfather Cleydon, and from a very early age he never let anything stand in the way of his determination to extract from life all the enjoyment it had to offer. People who knew the family well found it remarkable that the austere, single-minded William and his colourless, puritanical wife should ever have produced such a child. By his fifteenth birthday, Jonas had already succeeded in enticing to his bed more than one of the eager, full-breasted slave girls who worked in the Great House, and in the slave lines coarse,

good-humoured accounts of the young Master's latest esca-
pades circulated with laughter around the cooking fires in
the dying light of the evening.

Jonas was a natural horseman and a fine shot. Every
morning before sunrise he hunted along the river bank, and
the birds which fell to his gun were shared out among the
slave families as he rode through the lines on his way back to
the Great House for his breakfast. The children tumbled out
of their huts to salute him when they heard his horse
approaching: 'Marnin', Massa Jonas,' they called, 'Marnin', young baas.' He knew each one of them by name and
cheerfully returned their greetings as he passed by.

He still spent some of his time in the slave lines with the
boys he had played with as a child, but they treated him with
increasing deference as they all grew older and took their
own places in the fields of cane. Jonas recognised that the
gulf between them would, inevitably, grow wider with each
passing year; it was one of the few shadows that lay across
the full contentment of his life at New Providence.

When he was sixteen, Jonas quarrelled with his father for
the first time. Their argument was over the vexed question of
Abolition and William, thinking that his son's unacceptable
views had been shaped by his tutor, promptly dismissed the
young curate. He was hustled out of the house without
ceremony and placed on board the next merchant vessel
bound for England; and so Jonas's formal education came to
an abrupt end. But William Langford soon discovered that
the tutor's departure did not alter the opinions held by his
son, and the discovery deeply offended him.

'You are too young to know the difference between right
and wrong in this matter,' he declared to Jonas one morning
when the subject had once again raised its persistent head at
the breakfast table. 'The niggras are not like us. All they
want from life is food, a place to sleep and a black woman to
lie with – and that is what we give them.'

He pointed through the open window of the room towards

the black groom patiently holding his Master's mare at the front steps of the house.

'They need white men to tell them what to do,' he said. 'That is the only way they can be happy. It is when fools like that tutor of yours and the meddling missionaries fill their empty heads with mad ideas about freedom that they become fretful.'

With difficulty, Jonas reined in his own temper.

'You are wrong,' he replied quietly. 'They don't need anyone to inform them that their lives are hard or that the brand burns their skin. They know it well enough for themselves, and they know that only Abolition will cure it.'

'Come now, let us talk of other things . . .' his mother pleaded anxiously in an effort to bring peace to the table; but William would have none of it.

'You do not understand the matter,' he shouted furiously at his son. 'Do you believe that you can pull out the foundations of a house and still expect the walls to stand? Do you think that this estate could be run without slaves? Do you believe that we could live as we do if we ever gave the niggras freedom? Use the sense God gave you, boy.'

With an effort, he struggled to curb his anger.

'I should have listened to your mother,' he added in a quieter voice. 'I should have stopped you playing with the niggra children when you were small. It has spoiled your judgement, because now you think that they are like us.'

He left his coffee untouched upon the table and stamped out to snatch the reins of his horse and his leather riding crop from the hands of the anxious groom. The horse shied suddenly and the groom allowed the crop to fall to the ground. The unhappy man scrambled to retrieve it; William waited until he was on his knees and then kicked him hard on the buttocks. The groom endured the blow without a sound; his Master hauled himself into the saddle and rode off.

In the breakfast room, Jonas waited until the echo of the horse's hooves was lost in the distance; then he took up his gun from the hall and set off to shoot duck on the river and to quench the fire of his anger. But the sharp words exchanged between father and son had been overheard by a house slave in the passage outside the room. By evening they had been reported back to the black men and women around the cooking fires and soon every slave on the estate knew that, in spite of the colour of his skin, young Massa Jonas was on their side in the struggle for freedom.

As the issue of Abolition increasingly came to dominate the life of every Cecilian, both black and white, William Langford began to take an active part in the effort to oppose it. He had found little in common with his white colleagues in the past, but the impending crisis inexorably drew together all the planters of the island. William began to attend their monthly meetings at Mantara Bay, the second town of Saint Cecilia around which were loosely grouped most of the largest estates. He grew into the custom of taking his wife with him and, to his own considerable surprise, the blunt and forceful manner with which he expressed his views proved so popular with his fellow planters that by the beginning of 1830 no gathering of anti-Abolitionists was thought complete without him.

The experience of general approbation was entirely new to William. In the past, on other topics, none of his peers had ever troubled to seek his opinion; now they were willing to travel thirty miles on horseback to listen to what he had to say. He began to enjoy the experience. The measures which he publicly urged should be taken to keep the restless slaves in their place became increasingly harsh and uncompromising, and the slaves themselves took quiet note of what he said and marked him down as an implacable enemy.

On New Year's Day 1832, William and his wife left New Providence to attend yet another gathering of planters at Mantara Bay. They rode together across the spine of green mountains that divided the south of the island from the north, their personal slaves following at a respectful distance with the pack mule bearing their luggage. The meeting had been called to draft a message to the Governor in the capital about the conduct of the Baptist missionaries in the western parishes. During the course of their Sunday sermons, so it was said, these gentlemen were now openly inciting the slaves to claim their freedom. Some had gone so far as to urge the slaves to withhold their labour after the cane harvest and so allow the reaped stalks to wither in the fields. William Langford had been one of those chosen to address the meeting and to sign the message to the Governor.

William and his wife stayed two days at Mantara Bay as guests of a wealthy planter whose own splendid Great House stood on the crest of a hill above the harbour. On the evening of their arrival, from the comfort of wicker chairs laid out on the wide verandah of the house, they looked down upon a gathering of square rigged merchant ships at anchor on the pale green water of the bay. The ships were taking on sugar for Europe from a score of lighters ranged about them; but the tranquil, reassuring scene did not mirror the mood of the assembled planters in the town that weekend. Among them there was only one topic of conversation and that concerned the growing insolence of their slaves and the treason of the missionaries who encouraged it.

At the meeting in the old court house the following morning, tempers ran high; for all the brave words there was an undercurrent of fear which gave rise to ill-considered propositions. The few moderate men present were howled down before they could speak.

At the close of the first session, one sweating, apoplectic planter hauled himself to his feet and yelled: 'Enough of this talk and talk. The root of the trouble is to be found in the chapels of the missionaries. You know it, I know it. To hell with the message to the Governor; it will do nothing for us. I say we must burn the chapels to the ground and hang those who use them to instigate rebellion.'

64

The man paused to catch his breath and to give emphasis to his words.

'On my land,' he bellowed, 'we are accustomed to rid ourselves of rats by putting fire to their nests.'

The outburst was greeted with a general roar of approval; for a brief moment William Langford was able to hope that the assembled men could indeed be persuaded there and then to march off and raze the nearest Baptist chapel. If that happened, he intended to take his place in the front rank.

The violent mood subsided, however; attention returned to the wording of the message. It was tacit recognition of the fact that at the end of the day the Governor held all the cards; he alone could command the regular troops in Queenstown, whose presence on the island was the only factor that still held the restless slaves in check.

The proposed message was watered down to remove the more offensive passages, a perfunctory paragraph was added expressing loyalty to the distant king and pointedly trusting that he would not be ill-advised by his servants in parliament; then it was signed by every man present. Two of the younger planters were delegated to deliver it in person to His Excellency at his residence in the capital.

The meeting drew to an end in the afternoon and, one by one, the planters returned to their estates by carriage or on horseback. William and his wife, who had further to travel than most, spent the night in Mantara Bay and were up at first light next morning. Their host was at his front door to wish them a pleasant journey.

'Take good care,' he advised them courteously. 'It rained last night in the mountains and you will find the track treacherous with mud.'

The sun rose as he spoke, dispersing the thin blanket of mist that hung in the folds of the valleys through which they would pass. William and his wife, followed by the slaves with the pack mule, set off for home. And at that very moment, in accordance with a plan that had successfully been kept secret from the white population of the island for more than two months, fifty thousand slaves were rising in rebellion on the estates all around them.

The Great Slave Revolt of 1832, as it came to be known in later years, was well planned and bravely led. It had been made possible by the rumour, spreading swiftly from one plantation to another, that in London the king in his mercy had already granted freedom to the slaves in all his colonies, but that the news had been deliberately suppressed by the planters. In those circumstances, it was plain to even the most faint-hearted slave that the only way to gain his freedom was to fight for it, as black men had fought in Haiti under Toussaint and Christophe forty years earlier.

The rebellious black tide swept over the western parishes of Saint Cecilia and those whites who could, fled before it to the protection of the militia in Mantara Bay, or took boat to the safety of the capital. The rebel leaders despatched bands of mutinous slaves to take possession of outlying estates, and one such group was sent over the mountains to seize New Providence. It was these men who, quite by chance, intercepted William and his wife as they returned home on the first day of the rising.

The ragged, barefoot column of slaves blocked the road at a narrow pass between two outcrops of limestone rock. William and Margaret were suddenly surrounded by a wild, gesticulating army of black men. His face flushed with rage, William attempted to force a path through them.

'Get back there,' he yelled, his words echoing from the face of the cliffs beside him. 'Go back to your Masters or you will hang for it.'

The mob was stilled; men stepped back instinctively at the sound of a white man's voice raised in command. The circle of rebels which had closed in about the horses hesitated; those at the front wavered and sought to retreat. For a moment, William thought he had cowed them. Then a bolder spirit from behind him shouted into the silence; 'Don' hold up now: dis is war. We-all mus' be free. Kill de Backra.'

Instantly the spell was broken. Black hands reached out and dragged William and Margaret down from their horses and rolled them together in the hot, choking dust of the roadway. The bright blade of a cutlass rose and fell, and that first blow served to release all the pent-up hatred and resentment of the rebellious slaves. The mob gave a collective, animal roar of triumph. There was a mad, savage scramble to hack at the twitching bodies sprawled in the dust, so that every man there could claim credit for the act and, later, could point with pride to the dark bloodstains on the blade of his weapon.

What had begun as a simple act of murder became a kind of blood ritual, binding the participants together and, in a curious fashion, exorcising that deep-seated sense of inferiority which was a product of their condition.

Then the rebel column re-grouped and continued on its way over the mountains to New Providence, elated by its success, more murder in its heart.

Jonas Langford was seated on the front verandah of the Great House oiling the barrel of his shotgun when the slave who had been leading his father's pack mule burst out of the fading evening light. In the tumult of the murder, the mule had bolted and the man had been able to slip away and race through the bush back to New Providence.

The slave fell exhausted at Jonas's feet. 'Massa Jonas,' he gasped, his chest heaving with fatigue and the horror of what he had witnessed, 'de slaves dem makin' war. Dem done kill de Massa an' de Mistress. Run now, Massa Jonas, for dem comin' for you an' dem right behin' me.'

Almost before the man had finished speaking, Jonas could hear their approach. They were singing a hymn taught them by the missionaries, but they had invested it with a rhythm of their own and the words had been modified to suit the purpose of the rebellion. Their voices caressed the lines that spoke of blood and fire and death to white men: the effect was one of infinite menace.

'Go hide yourself, Wellington,' Jonas said. 'Make sure they do not find you here. If they know you came to warn me, they will kill you too.'

The slave hesitated, then fled for his life.

Methodically, Jonas wiped the barrel of his gun clean of oil, loaded it with shot and placed it by the side of his chair. He blew out the lantern on the table in front of him and waited alone in the gathering darkness. A little ring of fireflies danced across the verandah on the late evening breeze. He suffered no fear, only a deep regret that he was going to die when there still remained so many of life's pleasures as yet untasted; at the same time he was seized by a cold fury towards those planters like his father whose blind intransigence had finally brought about the rising they had feared for so long and for which they were themselves responsible. As the din of the approaching rebel band grew closer, Jonas drew back the hammer of his gun and hauled himself upright in his chair. There was no moon, but the evening star was already bright in the blue-black vault of the sky. Then a very curious event took place.

From around every cooking fire at New Providence, as though at some inaudible command, little parties of black men and women left their places on the hard-packed earth and came together to form a single column which moved with deliberate haste in the direction of the Great House. Some of the slaves in the procession carried burning torches in their hands to light the way; all were armed with cutlasses. No one spoke; there was only the muffled tread of bare feet in the dust of the roadway and a common resolve.

When it reached the Great House, the column of slaves branched into two streams, one moving to the left, the other to the right. When the heads of the two streams reunited, the Great House was surrounded; a living black picket fence enclosed the building. The men and women stood with their backs to the house; the light from the burning torches glittered on the cutlasses strapped to their sides. Their leaders took up position at the foot of the curving sweep of the steps which led to the front verandah; chief among them in the dancing, flickering light Jonas could just make out the powerful figure of Zacky, his childhood friend, a man of twenty now.

The advancing rebel column was not far behind. It halted briefly at the bungalow occupied by the white book-keeper William had hired only a few months earlier; then the wild-eyed men continued their march up the avenue of palms towards the Great House. They seemed to Jonas to flow out of the pale darkness of the night like some giant, malignant serpent. There were two hundred slaves at New Providence strung out now around the house, and the rebels in their column outnumbered them by three to one.

The hymn singing abruptly died away; the sound was replaced by an eerie, incomplete silence. In the front rank of the rebels a man brandished something impaled upon a tall bamboo pole. Jonas looked and saw that it was the severed head of the white book-keeper; the light of the burning torches fell upon the bloodless face, the eyes propped open, staring vacantly into the night.

On the verandah, Jonas waited patiently for the moment of his own death, regretting that his pride would force him to make use of his gun before he died. He could feel no hatred for the rebel slaves; they were doing what they saw as necessary to gain their freedom, and he could not find it in his heart to blame them.

The long column of rebels halted a few yards short of the circle of slaves that surrounded the Great House. From his place in the darkness of the verandah, Jonas watched their leader approach Zacky at the bottom of the flight of steps. The night was suddenly brittle with the tension of the encounter. Sharp words of disagreement drifted up out of the darkness.

'Let us pass, brudder,' Jonas heard the rebel leader say. 'We come to kill de white boy. Is for you-all as well dat we do dis; black men mus' be free.'

'You-all done killing enough already,' Zacky replied quietly. 'What is done is done, but dis young Massa is on our side. Leave him be.'

The leader disagreed. 'All de white folks mus' die,' he replied stubbornly. 'Babylon mus' fall, like it say in de bible. Black men mus' rule here now.'

Zacky was not moved.

'Ah tell you again, brudder, de young Massa is wid us,' he repeated. 'No one goin' touch him.' He paused, and then to make his position entirely clear: 'If you-all want to kill him,' he said, 'den you mus' pass us first.'

The two men stared at each other in silence; the moment seemed to have no end. Somewhere down in the slave lines a dog barked once and was silent; then the rebel leader turned abruptly on his heel, strode back to his column and consulted with the other men at its head.

On both sides the slaves waited in the darkness, those with weapons nervously caressing the handles of their cutlasses. A hot gust of wind stirred the dust around them and brought to Jonas out of the night the sweet, familiar scent of jasmine from the garden beyond the front steps.

At last the rebel leader returned to the place where Zacky waited. The two men faced each other again in a soft-edged circle of light cast by a single sputtering torch.

The leader held up his hands, palms outwards. 'We nuh come here to shed de blood of black people,' he said simply. 'Too much spill already by de white man. We goin' leave de white boy wid you.'

A kind of whistling sigh passed through the ranks of the slaves on both sides. The column of rebels turned about and marched back the way it had come. From his place in the shadows, Jonas watched the glow of their torches fade into the night. When the barking of the estate dogs had ceased at last and it was clear that the rebels had really gone, the ring of his own slaves melted silently away in groups of three and four to return to their quarters in the slave lines. A thin drizzle began to fall silently upon the New Providence estate, unlocking the scent of the earth and overlaying with its own distinctive pattern in the dust of the roadway both the footprints of the rebel slaves and the blood of the murdered book-keeper.

At the conch shell's blast next morning the normal routine of the day was followed exactly as if nothing unusual had taken place; no one spoke of the events of the previous night. The body of the book-keeper was buried without fuss in the field behind his bungalow and, later in the day, the mutilated corpses of William Langford and his wife were carried to the estate by a party of the Militia sent out for that purpose from Mantara Bay. Jonas buried them together that same afternoon; when the funeral was over, he returned to the Great House with the knowledge that at the age of eighteen he was now Master of New Providence, and that to save his young life two hundred of his slaves, his human chattels, had been prepared to put their own lives in the balance.

In spite of its early gains, the Great Slave Revolt of 1832 did not succeed. It was confined to the western parishes of Saint Cecilia and the Governor acted swiftly to despatch regular troops from the garrison in the capital to put it down. The black slaves, armed only with billhooks and cutlasses, found themselves confronted by white veterans of Waterloo, equipped with field artillery. Their leader, a foreman slave called Ezekial Blunt, was taken alive and the whole grand design for a second Haiti collapsed in bloody ruins.

In the market place at Mantara Bay, a stout wooden boom was erected and more than a thousand rebellious slaves were hanged from it before the planters were satisfied that the lesson had been well taught. Then their long pent-up fury burst upon the hapless white missionaries who were charged with inciting it all. The night sky of the western parishes was lit up by flames from the burning chapels and six of the most radical missionaries were put on trial for their lives.

The great rising itself was a failure; but, ironically, it turned out to be the factor that finally persuaded the parliament in London that slavery would have to be abolished. Just before his death on the wooden boom at Mantara Bay, one of the condemned leaders of the rising said calmly to his executioners: 'You can take my life now; but you must know that my people will try again. You will get no rest until all slaves are free.' And if the evident truth of his words was still resisted by the planters of Saint Cecilia, no responsible person in London was prepared any longer to contest it.

So it came about that on 1st August 1832 the institution of slavery was abolished in every British possession. The planters of Saint Cecilia not only forecast their own economic ruin as a result, but loudly predicted their bloody murder by their former slaves at the moment of freedom. But there was no violence; the black population of the island chose instead to mark the day of their emancipation by flocking to the chapels which the missionaries had quietly raised again on the burnt-out ruins.

At New Providence, Jonas Langford went with them to the nearest chapel where the congregation knelt together to thank God, at last, for the precious gift of liberty.

5

For all his love of the good things of life, and his conviction that black men and women were no less human than white ones, Jonas Langford was quite as shrewd a planter as his father had been and a good deal more far-sighted. He had foreseen that when the slaves were freed there would be an immediate exodus of black labour from the plantations on the plains to the rugged, unclaimed land of the interior.

'Those estates which don't offer fair wages and decent accommodation will find themselves without enough men and women to work their land,' he had warned, and in the event he was proved right. At the same time, those planters who took his warning to heart – and made conditions on their estates sufficiently attractive to stem the exodus – immediately discovered an unsuspected fact: slavery, after all, had been a more expensive system than the employ-ment of free labour. In the hysteria of the decade which preceded Abolition, no one had taken the trouble to work it out.

The bitterness of those last years, however, had left indel-ible scars. Most freed slaves wanted only to escape the cane fields, the detested symbols of their former bondage. They slipped quietly away and walked up into the empty hills. There they carved out for themselves little terraced plots of earth which clung precariously to the steep contours of the hillsides overlooking the river valleys and the wrinkled sea far beyond them. They grew just enough in the stony soil to feed themselves and their families; and there they were safe at last from the endless cycle of labour in the cane fields and the harsh authority of their former Masters.

Among the small number of freed slaves who elected to leave New Providence was Zacky. Jonas had always known that he would go, and in a curious way he was glad. Zacky was not a man made for servitude on another man's land; his spirit was too big for that. It was fitting that he should be his own master at last.

On the morning of the day he was to leave for the mountains, Zacky called at the Great House to say goodbye to Jonas. The two men met at the foot of the steps that led up to the verandah, standing by chance on the very spot where Zacky had confronted the leader of the rebel slaves less than a year before.

'I goin' now, Massa,' he said simply, and Jonas just nodded and replied: 'I know, Zacky; it is time for that.'

Then Jonas did something that no slave owner could ever have done: he put his arms around the man and hugged him to his chest.

'Thank you, Zacky,' he said. 'Thank you for my life.'

They did not meet again.

Down on the plains, those estates which were unable to attract enough labour to work their land fell first into the hands of the money lenders and then were sold off to the highest bidder. By 1840, more than sixty properties had been abandoned on Saint Cecilia. From their eyries high in the mountains, the former slaves looked down upon decaying factories and encroaching bush where once there had been carefully tended fields and all the purposeful activity of prosperous estates.

But if they felt any satisfaction at what had come to pass, they kept it entirely to themselves.

In London, the British Government voted £20,000,000 to compensate the owners of slaves throughout the Empire for what they had been obliged to give up. With his own small share of this money, Jonas demolished the slave lines at New

Providence and replaced the palm-thatched, rat-infested huts with decent accommodation for his labourers. Having done that, he shrewdly set out to buy the best of the small estates that were then coming so cheaply on the market. Not long afterwards, he was the owner of more than fifteen thousand acres on Saint Cecilia.

Jonas Langford's new status as one of the most successful landowners on the island was soon recognised in a letter from the Governor's secretary. On his next tour of the western parishes, the letter informed him, His Excellency proposed to pay a visit to New Providence. It was hoped that Jonas would be able to accommodate the Governor and his party for the night.

The Governor of Saint Cecilia was known to choose his hosts with some care before setting off on his periodic tours of the colony, and letters of the kind were much sought after by socially ambitious planters and their wives. A visit from His Excellency conferred upon those who entertained him an enduring cachet.

Jonas Langford received his letter with mixed feelings, but he gave orders that the rooms to be used by the Governor and his aides should be stripped of their cobwebs and the dust of years and modestly refurbished.

The Governor was a bluff, retired Major General who, as a young subaltern, had served on Wellington's staff at Ciudad Rodrigo. He took to Jonas at once. Over a dinner of crab backs and stewed water fowl on his first evening at New Providence, he raised his well filled glass towards his host and boomed: 'These are difficult days for planters on this island, Sir. I admire the way you keep your labourers happy and make money at the same time. I have met few who seem to be able manage the trick.'

'That is because they do not see that the one is necessary to ensure the other, Excellency,' Jonas replied.

The Governor enjoyed his stay at New Providence and he prolonged it by a day in order to shoot blue-winged teal on the river with his host. Not long after the visit, Jonas received an invitation to dine at Government House in the capital; and after his undoubted success at that dinner, his place in Cecilian society was assured.

A handful of older planters, and some of the richer merchants, found it difficult at first to accept him as an equal at the dinner table because they knew that his father had once been no more than an impoverished peasant farmer, but their more practical wives, seeking as always a match for unmarried daughters, found the attraction of his wealth irresistible. And their daughters, entranced by his easy charm and his fair-haired good looks, were quite prepared to have him even if he were penniless.

Early responsibility had given Jonas a quiet self-assurance and a confidence in his own worth. He was not intimidated by the new world into which he found himself so swiftly catapulted; in fact, the affected manners and over-elaborate courtesy, and the slavish reaction to every reported change of fashion in distant London, caused him amusement which he took little trouble to conceal. He had no intention of settling down as a married man until much later in his life and, in the meantime, he intended to enjoy the charms of as many pretty women as he could bring to his bed – and there was never a lack of them in the circles in which he now moved.

From time to time, in the years that followed, his affairs were the cause of disagreeable scandal, and on one occasion, over the matter of another man's wife, he was taken aside by the Governor's lady and firmly rebuked.

'There is a limit, Mr Langford,' she admonished him, 'to what even this society will tolerate. I must insist that you be more discreet in your affairs of the heart . . .'

But Jonas turned upon her the full and charming warmth of his smile and the Governor's lady discovered, as had others before her, that it was impossible to be vexed with him for more than an hour at a time. By the end of the week both of them had forgotten all about his promise to mend his ways and he was once again a welcome guest at Government House.

On Christmas Eve in 1848, Jonas set out at sunrise to attend a ball at Government House the following day. He had been riding for some three hours when his journey was interrupted by a sudden, torrential rain storm. In a matter of hours the rivers all along the southern coast, swollen by the run-off from the slopes of the mountain range from which they sprang, burst their banks and flooded the unpaved roads that led to the capital. They were soon impassable even to a determined man on horseback.

Cursing himself for not having set off the previous day as he had originally planned, Jonas was forced to take shelter in a small coaching inn along the way. It was a place he knew well, at which he often broke his return journey from the capital for a meal of jack cravalle and sweet potatoes. The inn was owned by a middle-aged coloured woman who, over the years, had developed a special affection for the young Master of New Providence not least because, unlike many customers she knew, he always took the trouble to praise her cooking after he had enjoyed a meal at the place.

The woman was called Danielle; she came from a family of free coloureds who had fled from nearby Haiti when she was still a child in order to escape the murderous attentions of the Emperor Dessalines. The family had arrived in Saint Cecilia possessing only the clothes in which they were dressed, but they had brought with them across the channel their ancient, unshakable belief in the power of voodoo and the Gods of the West African forest. The family had been obliged to settle deep in the mountains which overlooked the southern coastal plain of Saint Cecilia, for only in that place was there still empty land to be cleared. It was there that Danielle had grown up.

Danielle's mother, the ancient, withered matriarch of the clan, never quit her mountain fastness even after her children, one by one, left to find work in other parts of the island. In her *tonnelle*, half hidden by the shadows of a grove of giant silk cotton trees and wedged in among their buttress roots, she continued to practise the secret rites of voodoo just as she had done in her native Haiti.

Jonas Langford was not a superstitious man. He was casually contemptuous of the common Cecilian resort to *obeah* for supernatural assistance, and he professed to care nothing for the more potent Haitian beliefs and those who practised them. It was all nonsense, he declared with his usual good humour. The black population of New Providence and of the other estates along the southern coast of the island took a different view, however: they lived in a world where the ubiquitous presence of malevolent spirits was as unquestioned as the need constantly to appease them. For those people, the ancient, brown-skinned woman of the mountains was a figure of huge importance in their lives.

Secretly, in the dead hours of the night, little parties of black men and women seeking good fortune, or perhaps a cruel vengeance, were accustomed from time to time to make their way up the precipitous mountain paths to the *tonnelle* of the Haitian *houngan*. There, beneath the bearded branches of the silk cotton trees, they knew that the Gods of West Africa, under the old woman's direction, could be persuaded to put fire into the heart of a reluctant lover or to bring swift and awful retribution upon an unsuspecting enemy.

Jonas was imprisoned by the unrelenting weather. He paced the narrow balcony outside his room; the rain drummed incessantly upon the shingled roof; the dun coloured water swirled and eddied about the stone foundations of the inn. As darkness fell, clouds of ravenous mosquitoes forsook their hiding places in the water-logged crab holes along the river banks and invaded every room. To escape the worst of their torture, Jonas was forced to take shelter beneath the

78

coarse linen sheets of his bed. In the morning, he woke hot, irritable and uncharacteristically at odds with life.

At the close of the second day, when it began to seem likely to him that the rain would last forever, Danielle came to his room to remove the tray of supper he had scarcely touched. His loss of appetite disturbed her.

'Massa,' she said soothingly, 'do not fret. De rain boun' to hol' up soon now. Everythin' mus' have an end, even dis storm.'

Jonas was sprawled upon his bed. 'I am bored, Danielle,' he complained peevishly. 'I am bored to death.'

The woman had no doubt what he required.

'Massa,' she announced, 'I goin' sen' my niece to please you. She livin' only a little while from here.'

Jonas was silent. He did not feel the need for a woman; he wanted only to move on. But Danielle was not discouraged.

'You goin' like her, Massa,' she continued. 'She name Illana, an' she skin pale like sugar.'

For the first time since the rains began, Jonas was heard to laugh.

'Like sugar?' he inquired carelessly. 'Then you better send her up with my coffee tonight . . .'

The mood passed. He lay down again upon the bed and turned his face to the wall. The woman snuffed out the candle in its brass holder and withdrew. She went down to her room, threw a cloak around her shoulders and prepared to go out into the rain.

Jonas was woken by a knock on the door of his room some minutes after midnight. He hauled himself reluctantly out of bed, lit the candle, fumbled for the latch and opened the door. Through eyes heavy-lidded with sleep he saw before him a girl with pale bronze skin and dark, rain-wet hair. She was standing in the doorway, a wooden tray in her hands.

Sleep had driven from his mind all memory of his conversation with Danielle earlier that night. They looked at each other in silence. He took up the candle from the table by

79

his bed and held it high so that he could clearly see the girl's face. She met his gaze calmly; she was unselfconscious, unafraid. The guttering flame of the candle, momentarily caught by the draught from the open door, was mirrored in the depths of her coal black eyes.

In a voice so soft and deep that Jonas scarcely heard the words, she said: 'I bring your coffee, Massa.'

Instantly Jonas recalled Danielle's promise.

'Come then, Illana,' he said. 'Let us make each other happy.'

He took the tray from her hands and led her to his bed. She was to share it with him for the next seventeen years.

The rain ceased at dawn next morning as abruptly as it had begun three days earlier. In the afternoon, when the water had receded from the land, Jonas returned to New Providence with Illana riding behind him on a borrowed horse. Next day he installed her in the Great House as his housekeeper, an arrangement so commonplace in those days that it stirred no comment among his friends. Most white bachelors had coloured housekeepers on Saint Cecilia, and some men who were married did the same.

But Jonas Langford's relationship with his particular coloured girl developed one unprecedented complication: he fell in love with her.

One morning six months later, Jonas was seated in his study examining the estate account books. A shadow fell across his desk; he looked up from his work and saw Illana framed in the doorway of his room. She had never come uninvited to his study before; it was something he had not encouraged.

'Well,' he said now with mock severity, 'and why do you hunt me down to my place of work?'

The girl made no answer; at once Jonas pushed aside the leather-bound books, took her by the waist and sat her on his knees. He cupped her breasts with his hands and kissed her on the lips.

'Well,' he inquired again, 'what brings you?'

The girl summoned up her courage. 'I have something to ask of you, my love,' she whispered. 'I beg you not to be vexed with me for telling it.'

Jonas kissed her again. 'If it is a new dress you want,' he promised, 'I will buy half a dozen of them for you next time I ride to town. I will choose them in six different colours to be sure that you are pleased . . .'

But Illana had not come to ask for clothes.

'I do not need dresses,' she replied quietly. 'You give me more than I can wear. It is a favour of a different kind I have in mind.'

'Then tell me,' Jonas commanded.

The girl shut her eyes and gripped his hands in both of hers.

'I want you to ride with me into the mountains,' she whispered. 'I want to take you to my grandmother.'

She leant forward, burying her head on his chest. Her dark, fragrant hair spilled over the front of his shirt. Jonas could feel her slim body trembling with the fear that he might refuse her. Touched by her distress, he put his hand beneath her chin and lifted her head so that he could see her face.

'But why, Illana?' he asked. 'Why, in heaven's name? What can the old woman give us that we do not already have? Can you think I do not love you?'

There was a long moment of silence.

'I will tell you the truth,' the girl said at last. 'I will not lie.'

She stood up to face him.

'Every day of my life since the moment I met you,' she said, 'I have lived in fear that the time may come when I lose you to a woman of your own kind. My grandmother can prevent such things; she can bind us together for ever.'

Jonas took time to consider his answer. He was irritated

81

that the girl should wish to involve him in such foolishness, but at the same time he was not unhappy that she should love him in that way.

'I will think about it,' he said at last. 'At this moment, I will not promise more than that.'

But only two days later, as she lay naked in his arms upon their bed, he said to please her as she had just pleased him: 'We will ride into the mountains tomorrow morning. It can do no harm, after all, and I wish you to be happy.'

They set out on horseback at dawn next morning, following the course of the track that snaked its way up from the cane fields of the coastal plain into the damp heart of the mountains.

The air began to lose its cloying heat as they climbed higher. Huge saman trees, their branches hung with bearded epiphytes, rose above the track; everywhere about them were stands of balasier with boat-shaped scarlet bracts hanging down to the ground. In the rain forest on either side of the track only a few pale bars of sunlight penetrated the deep shadow beneath the high canopy of leaves. A thin mist clung to the branches of the trees and curled in sombre patterns beneath them. A light rain began to fall upon the forest as they moved higher into the mountains; soon the run-off from the valley slopes raced across the course of the track in quicksilver streams of crystal water. Only the raucous cry of a jabbering crow and the muffled echo of the horses' hooves disturbed the brooding silence of the forest.

They arrived at the clearing among the grove of silk cotton trees as darkness was falling over the plain far below them. At one side of the clearing there was a simple wattle hut; in the centre stood the *tonnelle* Illana had spoken of. Jonas saw that it was a long, palm-thatched structure open on three sides; the hard-packed mud floor was chequered with dark, irregular stains. The stench of stale blood hung heavily on the air.

82

In the gloom at the far end of the *tonnelle* a very old woman was perched on a wooden stool waiting motionless for them to approach. She was a frail, bird-like creature; her pale brown face was incredibly wrinkled and furrowed, like the outer husk of a fallen coconut. Only her eyes were young, and they seemed to burn in that ancient visage with a strange and fearful incandescence.

The woman was wearing a shapeless robe which trailed on the ground and there was a turban of the same dirty white material wrapped tightly around her head. In the wider darkness behind her, at the very back of the *tonnelle*, Jonas could just make out the soft-edged shapes of a cluster of wooden cages and a large black coffin decorated with crudely rendered hieroglyphics. Before the coffin stood a wooden cross draped with a soiled morning coat and surmounted by a black top hat. He recognised it as the altar of Baron Samedi, chief of the legion of those who had passed on. He shivered a little in the damp air of the clearing.

Illana approached the old woman.

'*C'est moi, grandmaman*,' she called softly. '*C'est Illana*. I have brought a white Master with me to receive your blessing.'

The old woman grunted; she rose painfully from the stool. She did not appear surprised at their unheralded arrival; indeed, Jonas received the strong impression that in some curious way she had been expecting them.

'Come into the hut with me, Illana,' she commanded in the guttural French patois of her native Haiti. 'Leave M'sieur the white man here for a while.'

There were no chairs in the *tonnelle*, not even a bench. Jonas squatted uncomfortably on the floor and waited. In the valley below, the silence was broken by the sweet-melancholy call of a *siffleur montagne*. The shy bird's song was a series of clear whistles in phrases of two or three crystal notes, dropping more than an octave on the scale. The walls of the valley caught and amplified the sound. Somewhere nearby a rotten branch snapped with a report like a gunshot: the bird's song was cut short in mid-phrase. Jonas shivered again in the chill of the evening.

It was quite dark by the time the old woman returned to the *tonnelle* with Illana, a candle held in her hand. She motioned Illana to sit beside Jonas on the hard mud floor. From a place at the back of the *tonnelle* she withdrew a rusting sabre with a silver hilt; with the point of the weapon she described two circles in the dust of the floor.

From one of the cages, hidden now in darkness, she fetched two black cockerels. She trussed their legs with practised skill and threw one of the young fowls into the centre of each of the two circles. Employing the point of the sabre as a spade, she excavated a shallow channel in the mud floor, joining one circle to the other.

She took up a tall goatskin drum from somewhere in the shadows and beat out upon it a slow, erratic rhythm. She circled the floor of the *tonnelle* as she played, sideways like a crab; then, in a thin, cracked voice she began to sing: 'Venez mon Dieu', she chanted. 'Venez mon doux Sauveur, venez mon Dieu . . .'

She began to turn upon the floor, faster and faster as she speeded up the beat of the drum. Almost imperceptibly her invocation to the Saviour became a more strident plea to the ancient Gods of the forests of West Africa, the black Gods of her ancestors.

'Venez Mama Lwa,' she shouted. 'Venez Papa Legba; venez Ogoun Ferraile . . .'

One by one the Gods of voodoo were summoned from their homes on the African coast to that lonely *tonnelle* in the mountains of Saint Cecilia. As each dark divinity took possession of her frail body, the old woman emitted a piercing shriek of ecstasy.

The tall drum beat faster and faster, the *houngan* whirled in tighter and tighter circles around the wretched cockerels. Then, with a final yell of triumph, she fell to the floor beside

84

the circles she had drawn in the dust.

For a long moment there was silence in the *tonnelle*, broken only by the old woman's rasping, wheezing intake of breath. Then she picked herself up, squatted on her haunches and addressed Illana.

'Tell this white man you have brought here,' she said in patois, 'tell him that now I join the two of you together. Tell him that it is not like a marriage that the white priests make; tell him that this bond cannot be broken with impunity. It is made through me by the Gods of our homeland and no human being can set aside their compact without punishment.'

The old woman hauled herself stiffly to her feet.

'Let him know,' she said, 'that if ever he seeks to take another woman, death shall find him out.'

She reached out and touched the black sleeve of Baron Samedi, so that her meaning should be quite clear.

The flame of the guttering candle was drawn out by a passing gust of wind. The old woman's shadow danced crazily across the thatched ceiling of the *tonnelle*; her formidable personality appeared to expand to fill the frail building. Jonas suddenly found it difficult to breathe; an insufferable weight seemed to have fallen about his shoulders, forcing the breath from his lungs. He wanted to get up, to walk out into the cool night air, to recover his balance and composure, but his legs had lost their strength. He glanced sideways at Illana; her eyes were closed.

The old woman began a sacred incantation.

'Lade immenenou daguinin soilade naguignaminsou . . . pingolo, pingolo, roi monter nous la prie qui minin Africain . . . Oh! Oh! Oh! . . .'

The incantation was repeated several times; to Jonas it seemed to last for ever. Then it was finished. There was a moment of utter silence. With a shriek which lifted Illana out of her state of trance, the old woman flung herself from the place where she was standing and grabbed the trussed cockerels by their necks. There were two audible cracks as the vertebrae snapped beneath her fingers. From somewhere within the folds of her robe she drew a knife; with two swift strokes she decapitated both fowls. The headless bodies twitched and jerked frantically within the circles drawn to contain them in the dust. The scarlet blood spouted from the stumps of their necks and ran across the circles to fill the little excavation which connected them. The blood from the two circles mingled and then overflowed on to the earth of the *tonnelle* floor.

Jonas looked up at the face of the old woman. In the pale light of the guttering candle it was covered in sweat; the eyes were as red as the blood of the fowls. Then, without warning, the strength seemed to ebb from her frail body.

Addressing Illana, in a voice that was scarcely now more than a whisper she said: 'It is done, grandchild. He is yours. Tell him that he can desert you now only on pain of death. I wish you happiness.'

She collapsed on the floor of the *tonnelle*, brittle as an autumn leaf in her exhaustion, and almost instantly she was asleep.

By the light of a three-quarter moon, Jonas and Illana returned cautiously down the track that snaked through the rain forest back to the familiar plains of New Providence. They reached the outlying cane fields of the estate just as the rising sun scaled the summit of the mountain range behind them, and those black labourers who witnessed their return averted their eyes and took care not to voice their thoughts about where the couple might have journeyed – and to what purpose.

6

Jonas Langford abandoned the social life which turned about the formal receptions and the lavish dinner parties held at Government House. It was not that the invitations ceased, but as they could never include Illana he found no pleasure in accepting them. 'If she cannot sit at table with me,' he said, 'then I have no wish to eat.'

At first, his friends had taken it for granted that his infatuation would prove merely another passing fancy. He was not the first white man to succumb to the charms of a beautiful brown girl; but as everyone well knew, in due course the reality of the situation always asserted itself over the physical pleasure, no matter how sweet. The coloured mistresses eventually were pensioned off and, in good time, the erring men married girls of their own colour.

As the months turned to years at New Providence, however, it was admitted by even the most sceptical observer that this affair was different: Jonas Langford had no intention of abandoning Illana. His love for her grew only stronger with time. At last, even the most optimistic mothers reluctantly crossed his name off their private lists of desirable sons-in-law and looked about them for less attractive but more conventional victims.

Jonas relinquished his position in society without regret. He maintained links only with his oldest friends, who understood his passion for Illana and who, secretly, envied him his lovely coloured girl.

The years that followed were the happiest of his life. He had Illana and he had the pleasant occupation of overseeing his estates, scattered now throughout the island. He visited them regularly, always taking Illana with him in his open buggy for he could not bear to be separated from her for even a single night. Her presence meant, of course, that he could never stay with his white friends, but there was a house on each of his properties and they lived together in one of these whenever they were away from New Providence.

For Saint Cecilia itself, however, those same years were full of difficulty and disquiet. The freed black population expanded rapidly; soon, the little plots of land which so many of them had carved out of the mountain sides were no longer able to sustain all the former slaves and their children. Unemployment spread like a pestilence and with it hunger and discontent. The gift of freedom by itself had not proved sufficient.

The discontent was most marked in the eastern parishes of the island, far from New Providence but where, in 1857, Jonas had impulsively bought another small, bankrupt property. He had done what he could to develop the place and to provide work for as many men and women as possible, but the soil was poor and the yield of sugar never paid the wages of the labourers.

In October 1865, Jonas Langford left New Providence to offer the property as a gift to the local Council for the settlement of black peasants with no land of their own. Warned by a friend of the hostile mood of those who could find no work in the area, he left Illana at home, disregarding for once the tears with which she begged him to take her.

He arrived in the parish to find a note from the Chief Magistrate informing him that there was trouble at hand and asking him to meet the Council in the Court House at the nearby town of King Charles Bay the following morning. And so it came about that, next day, Jonas rode into the town only to be caught up in the bloody drama that was to become known as the King Charles Bay rebellion and which was effectively to change the course of the history of Saint Cecilia.

In the tense weeks before Jonas's arrival in the town, a hungry band of peasants led by a man called Cudjoe Baines had walked forty miles to the capital to present a list of grievances to the Governor. The Governor refused to see them. Instead, he sent out a message from the room where he was taking his luncheon: 'Return at once to your homes. The solution to your problems lies in hard work on your land, not in insolent complaint.'

So none of them was able to explain to the Governor that the chief of their grievances was the fact that they had no land to work. By the time they had returned to their villages, tired and desperate, a decision had been taken at Cudjoe Baines's insistence to march in force upon the local Council at its sitting in King Charles Bay next morning.

To the Chief Magistrate and his colleagues closeted with Jonas Langford in the Court House that day, news of the approach of a wild, belligerent mob of black peasants called for stern measures. The local militia of fourteen white men was turned out. The mob filled the square at the front of the Court House and overflowed up the main street of the town.

The Chief Magistrate climbed on to the little wrought-iron balcony of the building and, cupping his hands to his mouth to make himself heard, instructed the excited, gesticulating gathering of men and women to disperse. His words were lost in an angry tumult. Pale with rage he ordered his Clerk to bring him a copy of the Riot Act; he read it aloud in order to justify the action he was now determined to take, but this time the sense of his hurried words was lost even to the white men who stood close behind him. The mob was not intimidated; led by Cudjoe Baines, men began to press forward towards the steps of the Court House. The Chief Magistrate gave a sharp command, the little band of part-time soldiers put their carbines to their shoulders; the mob pressed forward again and the soldiers fired into its front rank. Eight black men fell dead in the dust of the cobbled square. The report of the carbines was followed by an eerie moment of silence, broken only by the agonised cry of a man who had taken a bullet in the groin; then the mob gave voice to a strange animal roar, not of fear but of anger. The soldiers turned to re-load their weapons, but it was suddenly apparent to everyone there that it was too late for that; the Court House was going to be stormed, the Militia would be overwhelmed by sheer numbers and the white men inside the building were going to be killed.

It took time, however. The rioters surrounded the building; then, with the approach of evening, they set it on fire. As the desperate men inside broke out to escape the flames, they were cut down one by one in the cobbled square. Cudjoe Baines himself despatched the Chief Magistrate with a single blow of his cutlass. Of the twenty-seven white men inside the building, only four escaped. Two were local doctors; one was the cunning vicar who knew of a hidden exit through a cellar; and the last was Jonas Langford.

For many years after the bloody incident, people were to wonder whether Jonas had been permitted to escape with his life because his sympathies were well known. But in the wild confusion of the moment, with the moonless night lit up by the blood-red flames of the burning Court House and the air full of the cries of men falling beneath the cutlass blows of the incensed mob, it may have been no more than good fortune. He himself could never decide afterwards whether his escape had been sanctioned or whether it was blind chance that allowed him to drop unseen from a rear window of the building, concealed at the critical moment by a swift eddy of smoke, and to make his way down to the sea. There at the water's edge he took shelter within the thick foliage of a sea grape tree until a party of marines, despatched from Queenstown by the Governor, landed on the beach from their frigate next morning.

The Governor suppressed the abortive rebellion with a savagery so extreme that it led eventually to his recall. More than four hundred of the wretched, landless peasants were summarily hanged from a gallows erected in the shadow of the gutted Court House and their bodies flung into a hastily excavated trench beside it. Cudjoe Baines, leader of the insurrection, was raised to the yard arm of the frigate anchored in the bay and died slowly there, kicking and flailing wildly in his agony as the noose tightened inexorably about his throat. On shore, more than a thousand men and women who had demonstrated support for the rebels were flogged insensible.

But there was to be a more fateful consequence than the deaths of four hundred men. In the capital, the spineless white legislature, terrified by the thought that the uprising might be part of a wider conspiracy to create a second Haiti, surrendered their right to rule themselves and petitioned the British Government to accept that responsibility. So it was that in 1866, Saint Cecilia ceased to govern itself and became a Crown Colony administered by an alien parliament three thousand miles away in London. Almost alone among the planters of the island, Jonas Langford's voice was raised in protest; it was lost in the tumult.

The seven hours he had spent in the besieged Court House, under what he had been sure was a sentence of death, left their indelible mark upon Jonas. The experience had been a rude intimation of his own mortality. He was fifty-one years old and, like his father, he had been inclined to give little thought to the matter of providing an heir to his property. In the past there had always seemed to be time for that later in his life. Now it had become an issue he could no longer bring himself to ignore.

Jonas decided that he must marry at once and produce a son. The marriage, as he saw it, would alter nothing between himself and Illana. Had she been white, he would, of course, have married her; but the hard fact was that in spite of his love for her – and his genuine affection for black people in general – Jonas could not bring himself to father children with African blood in their veins. Deep down within himself, at the core of his being, the old prejudices were just as firmly rooted as in any other white West Indian.

Of course he made excuses for it all: on Saint Cecilia, he told himself, coloured people were still second class human beings. He was sorry it was so, but he could not ignore the fact. He was the owner of great estates; it was necessary, when the time came, that they should be inherited by a son who could take his place as an equal among the other white families of the island. It was necessary to see things as they were.

But that was not the real reason he would not father a coloured heir and, secretly, he knew it.

The marriage he now wished to contract was to be an acknowledged affair of convenience. His wife's sole duty would be to bear him an heir; after that she must go her own way. He would settle enough money upon her to keep her in comfort for the remainder of her life in another country. The child, and he never doubted that it would be a son, would remain at New Providence to be brought up under his own supervision.

In the event, it did not prove difficult to find a white woman of suitable background willing to accept these conditions. The lady was a large, good-natured Englishwoman, the widow of a Captain in one of the British infantry regiments stationed in Queenstown who had been carried off by yellow fever the previous year. He had left his wife without an income.

Her first meeting with Jonas was brisk and businesslike. The main features of the intention were discussed and agreed; the size of the ultimate settlement was proposed and accepted; and it was arranged that she would return to England alone one year after bearing the child. It would give her time to train a black nanny to look after the boy when she had gone.

'I shall not wish you to see the boy after that,' Jonas told her. 'And you and I shall not meet again. If you wish for a divorce after your return to England then I shall be glad to arrange it. For myself, I shall not marry again.'

'Very well, Mr Langford,' the woman replied quietly. 'I find that acceptable. I agree to the proposal.'

Jonas saw no need to confide his plan to Illana until two weeks before the wedding was to take place. He explained it all to her then as nothing more than a business transaction, a matter of expediency quite devoid of any emotional commitment, and he took it for granted that she would see it in the same light. It would alter nothing between them, and it would provide a solution to the one problem that cast a shadow across the enjoyment of his life with her.

'You will come to love the boy,' he said confidently, 'because he will be part of me.'

Illana made no answer; so that he should not see the swift rush of tears, she turned her face away from him. When she came to his bed as usual that night, so skilfully did she conceal her own heartbreak that even in the act of love Jonas failed to detect the smallest sign of the grievous wound he had inflicted upon her.

The wedding itself was a brief affair held at dusk in the drawing room of the Great House. Apart from Jonas and his bride, there were present only his two white overseers to serve as witnesses, and the local parson.

As soon as the ceremony was over and the parson had been ushered out, Jonas led his bride to their bed. He was anxious to lose no time in fathering the son he required so that the woman might return to England and Illana resume her rightful place in his house. It was a joyless coupling.

He was woken by his groom before first light next morning. The distraught man, ignoring every unwritten rule of conduct, burst into the house while the servants still slept and hammered at the door of his Master's bedroom.

Drugged with sleep, Jonas left his bride in the bed and went to the door. The groom stood there, his eyes rolling with fear, his sweatstained straw hat crushed flat between his black hands.

'In God's name,' Jonas demanded thickly, 'what is it at this hour, Lijah?'

The man fell to his knees; he clutched at the sleeve of Jonas's nightshirt.

'Massa,' he whispered, his voice trembling with a terrible anguish, 'It Miss Illana. She dead.'

She had waited until the wedding was over and night had come down across the land. Then she had left the room which Jonas had assigned to her on the ground floor and climbed the grass-quilted slope behind the house. There she had flung herself naked into the cold, crystal water of the pool beneath the spring which issued from a cleft between two granite rocks.

From the place where she had stood beside the pool she would have seen the window of the bedroom to which Jonas had taken his bride; she would have seen the lamp flame die in the moment before he turned to her to consummate their marriage. He had gone back, after all, to a woman of his own colour, just as she had always feared he would, and the hurt was too great to be endured.

Nine months later to the day, Jonas's wife produced the heir he had wished for; but it took more than three days before anyone at New Providence could find the courage to tell him that he had a son. He was overwhelmed by a burden of guilt and anguish so unbearably heavy that even people who had known him all his life were now scarcely able to recognise him. He wandered aimlessly about his estate, seeing no one, eating nothing, caught up in the toils of a terrible nightmare of the spirit. Occasionally, he would mount his horse and gallop blindly into the hills behind the house, returning wild-eyed and incoherent long after darkness had fallen over his land. His life no longer held purpose or direction.

Two weeks after Illana's death, he discovered on the verandah outside his bedroom a mud-stained paper package tied up with a length of mountain liana. He stripped away the paper: inside was a crudely modelled clay figurine of a man he recognised as himself. Protruding from the figure's stomach there was a sharp wooden needle. He knew at once what it meant: he was not to be granted the swift, merciful end that was always signalled by a needle through the heart. For him, Baron Samedi had seen fit to ordain a slower, more agonising departure to the distant place reserved for those unwise enough to violate a voodoo compact.

Jonas Langford's son was christened Charles, but the boy's own father did not attend the perfunctory baptismal ceremony and, indeed, could scarcely bring himself to look at his son. There was nothing left in his twilight world capable of affording him either comfort or release. Then, on the morning of the first anniversary of Illana's death, he reached a decision: he resolved to build another Great House at New Providence.

The new building would be the most splendid structure on Saint Cecilia; it would be larger than the Governor's residence in the capital and its decoration would be finer than that of the old cathedral which stood beside it. There is no evidence that Jonas had ever heard of Shah Jehan and the story of the Taj Mahal, but there can be no doubt that in his inconsolable grief he conceived the new house as Illana's memorial, binding her forever – but too late – to his own family in the only way that was left to him.

He raised the building over the spring in which she had drowned herself, so that in every room on the ground floor there would be heard the musical rush of water beneath the mahogany floorboards. The design was his alone. Because it was constructed on the slope of a hill, the house stood taller at the front than at the back. The building was rectangular in shape; the gabled roof was supported at the front by an elegant series of tall marble columns and a balustraded double staircase swept up from the gravelled courtyard to meet the marble floor of the verandah. From the head of these steps there was an uninterrupted view of the distant sea across wide green lawns split down the middle by the quicksilver course of the stream which issued from beneath the building. In time, the fluted balustrades which flanked the steps were lost under a cloak of white and purple bougainvillea and delicate stands of the night-blooming cereus wrapped themselves about the base of each marble column. On still evenings, the fragrance of their short-lived blossoms filled the house.

The entrance from the front verandah led directly to a vast hall, capped by a glazed cupola set high in the roof. The polished marble of the floor had been quarried from the mountains; the walls were panelled in fine-grained mahogany felled on the estate. A cedar staircase at either side of the hall led to the wings of the upper storey and the bedrooms.

At the back of the hall, perpetually cast in shadow, was the spring which gushed from the cleft in the granite rocks. Jonas left it, and the pool into which the water fell, untouched. The families of little whistling frogs, which lived among the rocks at the margin of the pool, did not desert their home when it was enclosed by the building: at night, the high-pitched melody of their mating song echoed about the marble hall and drifted down the long, empty corridors of the house.

The building was approached by an avenue flanked by two splendid rows of royal palms. The walls were painted white from the eaves to the ground; from the deck of a ship passing along the distant coast, it seemed to glow with a curious incandescence against the dark green hills behind it. It was a house inspired by a great love, and Jonas named it Illana's Hall.

On the evening of the day the building was completed, he

ordered the old one destroyed by fire, and from the steps of Illana's Hall he watched alone as the tall flames consumed the empty rooms haunted by her memory.

Jonas Langford died at Illana's Hall in 1875. He had lingered on for eight barren, desolate years after the death of Illana. In this miserable twilight of his life he was a recluse on his estate, never visiting any of his scattered properties, never seeing even his oldest friends, rarely speaking to another human being. He appointed an attorney to take charge of what he owned and he never again troubled even to glance at the account books which were laid out upon his study desk for inspection at the end of every quarter. At night, long after everyone else had gone to bed, he could be heard pacing the floor of his room like a caged and desperate animal. The vengeance of Baron Samedi had proved every inch as cruel as the old *houngan* had once warned it would be.

To his son, he was a remote, forbidding figure. In later years Charles Langford found it impossible to reconcile the accounts he was given of Jonas as a young man – carefree, charming, in endless pursuit of pleasure – with the grey, grim-faced parent he could remember for himself.

Catherine, Jonas's wife of convenience, stood by him after Illana's death. Whatever could be said about the circumstances of her marriage, she proved to be a compassionate woman, and if she ever regretted that fateful agreement, she took care never to let anyone know it.

Three weeks after Jonas died, she left the estates in the charge of the attorney he had retained and returned at last with her son to England.

7

Charles Langford was seven years old when he arrived in London with his mother in the winter of 1875. Catherine bought a house overlooking the common at Wimbledon and, when he was ten years old, Charles was despatched to a boarding school for the sons of gentlemen in the Berkshire countryside. He remained there until he was eighteen and old enough to go up to Oxford: by that time his childhood memories of Saint Cecilia had almost faded from his mind. In every apparent way he was no different from any other middle-class English boy of the same age.

His mother chose the day before he left for his University to tell him for the first time about his father's affair with Illana. The information did not come entirely as a shock to him; he had always known that there was something very curious about the nature of his parents' marriage. But he found hard to bear the knowledge that his mother had once been prepared, for a sum of money, to abandon him when he was one year old, and the truth left its mark upon him.

His father's conduct – in particular his love for a coloured woman – he found even more unforgiveable and deeply shaming. At his boarding school in Berkshire it was common knowledge among the boys that Negroes were just a short step removed from the higher apes: you only had to look closely at a gorilla's features for the fact to become obvious. He cringed at the thought of what he would have been subjected to had they learnt that his father had loved one of the creatures.

To his mother he said only: 'I am sorry for what happened to you, but I shall never understand how you could have entered into that agreement in the first place.'

'No,' she replied. 'I would not expect it. I can only tell you that at the time there seemed no other way. The world is not kind to penniless widows.'

They never spoke of the matter again.

Charles Langford returned to Saint Cecilia to claim his estates in the summer of 1890; he was twenty-two years old. By that time he was a polished young man of the world, the first member of the Langford family who would have passed anywhere as an English gentleman, and he retained for the rest of his life the exaggerated accent and the formal, slightly pompous middle-class English manners of the period. People who knew nothing of his background were always astonished to learn that his grandfather had been a barely literate West Indian peasant, a fact that Charles took great pains to conceal whenever he could.

His mother did not return to the West Indies with her son. Not surprisingly, her own memories of New Providence were profoundly unhappy and she had succeeded in making for herself in London the kind of comfortable, secure life that she had originally sought. Although she kept in touch with Charles by letter, they never saw each other again after his departure for Saint Cecilia. She died suddenly on Christmas Eve in 1908. In his diary, her son recorded the news of her death in a single paragraph:

'News today,' he wrote, 'that Mama passed away on the 24th of last month. She had been willing to trade her infant son for a sum of money, which I find hard to excuse in her.'

On his arrival at New Providence, it had naturally been expected that Charles would take over the management of his estates from the hands of the attorney who had looked after them since the year of Illana's death, but it was soon apparent that he had no intention of doing any such thing. He could see no merit in making work for himself when he

99

could perfectly well afford to pay someone else to do it for him. He was by nature an indolent man and the role of gentleman of leisure, which he soon adopted, appeared to suit him very well. He became the first member of his family in the West Indies effectively to separate himself from the black population of the islands. He was also the first of a new class of white West Indian, insulated by wealth from anything that wearied or displeased them, rich enough no longer to need to take a personal interest in the source of their wealth. Charles's grandfather had been abominably cruel to his slaves. He had whipped them and branded them, but always he had lived with them and amongst them, and was as much a part of their lives as they were part of his. He had eaten much the same food as they ate, and suffered the same illnesses – for malaria and yellow fever were no respecter of persons.

In his energetic pursuit of pleasure, William's son Jonas had shown that he was made of different stuff, for he loved the good things of the world that money could buy: rich clothes, fine harness, choice wines. But, in spite of all this, he too lived in the closest everday contact with the black men and women he employed. He could call each one by name, he knew the age of every child, he was aware of all their individual virtues and vices. He recognised their quick good humour; their generosity of spirit; their unspoken hatred of those they perceived to hate them; their warm response to friendly gestures; their sly cunning; their love of children, black and white; their unshakable loyalty to those they trusted; their scandalous promiscuity. Like his father before him, he knew the characteristic pungent smell of their sweating bodies as well as he knew that of his own.

In many respects, both William and Jonas Langford knew more about the black men and women they lived amongst than they knew about those of their own race. They would have greeted with derision the absurd idea that they should somehow separate their lives from those of their black employees. They both knew in their different ways that the destinies of black and white men in the West Indies were inextricably intertwined, and would always be so no matter what else changed.

Charles Langford, on the other hand, saw the matter in an entirely different light. To him, the educated English gentleman, black Cecilians were alien creatures. They were dirty and untrustworthy, and it was abundantly clear, as he had been told at school, that they lacked all the finer instincts of a civilised race; they were, in short, a lesser kind of human being. He employed them as servants in his house, and his own well-being required their labour in his fields, but as individual men and women they were of no real consequence. So complete in his mind was his separation from them, so great the margin of his superiority, so far above them his position, that after a while he became scarcely more aware of the existence of his labourers than of his cattle in the fields. They were shadows in the background of his life. It was a development that would have astonished and baffled the earlier generations of his family.

In the third year after his return from Europe, he suddenly resolved to write an account of his family's history in the West Indies. It was clear from the start that the project would entail a considerable effort, but in those early years he felt the need to occupy his days, since no aspect of the management of his properties in any way stirred his interest. There was another, stronger motive, however: just as he had separated himself from the black men and women of his estates, so now he wished to distance himself from the uncouth generations who had struggled with their hands in the soil to build the fortunes of his own family. He was secretly ashamed of his humble origins – of the fact that his grandfather had once been no more than a semi-literate peasant grubbing in the earth, and that his father was a lecherous man who had loved a coloured woman. The awareness that everyone on Saint Cecilia knew very well from where he had sprung, that his own polished, urbane manners could never alter the nature of his antecedents, troubled him deeply. The act of writing The Journal, as he called it, was a kind of private catharsis; in a curious way, it enabled him to come to terms with the facts that shamed him and, having confronted them in this form, to put them out of his mind.

To capture as accurately as he could the details of his family's early years in the West Indies, first in Barbados and then in Grenada, Charles spent several weeks in each island.

In Barbados, he discovered that the estate on which his ancestor Cleydon had served his ten-year sentence of hard labour was still in the hands of the descendants of the family that had owned it in those distant days. The estate factory was in ruins, however, and the whole property was run down and ill-kept. The owner and his wife turned out to be a shabby couple, with little money and no faith in their future on the island.

They escorted Charles around their exhausted land with much ceremony. They walked with him up to the northern border of their property, to a little limestone church which overlooked the sea and, in the distance, the place where Cleydon, the first West Indian Langford, had lived with his woman upon the golden beach. In his Journal, Charles compared his own prosperity with their pathetic condition, and he wasted no sympathy on them because he knew that their forebears had spared none for Cleydon.

In Grenada, Charles found that the land which lay in the palm of the river valley, once so lovingly tilled by his great-grandfather Robert, had been abandoned for many years and so had reverted once again to the Crown. It was in much the same wild state in which Robert had first seen it. Charles spent a week scrambling about in the matted undergrowth, armed with a sketch map and a compass, until eventually he was able to trace the post holes of the modest wooden house which Robert had raised there for his family in 1767, and which had been burnt to the ground by the marauding French soldiers who had taken the island twelve years later.

On Saint Cecilia itself, the job of collecting information about his family was far easier; there were people still living who could remember his grandfather William, and there was the material stored in the Colonial Archives and in the various parish registers.

As soon as the task was finished and the last word had been written, he sealed the leather-bound note book in a stout manila envelope and locked it away at the back of the iron safe in his study. He never once opened the envelope again for the rest of his life: the catharsis was successful.

Under the shrewd care of the old attorney, New Providence and its satellite estates prospered at the close of the nineteenth century. By the time of the Queen's death in 1901, it was generally conceded that Charles Langford was one of the three most wealthy men on Saint Cecilia. In 1910, this fact was recognised by an invitation to him to serve on the Governor's Privy Council, with the undemanding duty to give advice when it was sought and the right to style himself 'the Honourable' Charles Langford.

The family, as he reflected with satisfaction on the day of the appointment, had come a long way from the barren, salt-poisoned plot of land on which Robert and his wife had settled in Saint Cecilia, and immeasurably further still from the foetid hold of the ship which had transported Cleydon Langford to Barbados as a wretched convict more than two hundred years earlier.

Immediately after the abortive uprising of 1865, which had so nearly cost Jonas Langford his life and put an end to the story of the family in the West Indies, Saint Cecilia entered upon a period of unfamiliar tranquillity. It was almost as if, exhausted by the turbulent conflicts of earlier times, the island had suddenly fallen asleep. The occasional visitor who strayed off the well beaten path from Europe to South America, and who somehow found himself on Saint Cecilia, invariably remarked upon the dream-like quality of life which seemed to cocoon the beautiful island and its people. It had slipped imperceptibly out of the mainstream of West Indian history into a placid Caribbean backwater. Successive British Governors came and went at five-yearly intervals, leaving no more evidence of their passage than a paved street bearing their name in some remote and sleepy coastal township.

In many respects, the course of Charles Langford's own life was all of a piece with this curious period in the history of the island. It was comfortable and it was free from anxiety, but it was entirely uneventful. Compared with the lives of the West Indian Langfords who had preceded him, it was also unimaginably dull. Apart from his occasional duties as a Privy Councillor, he had nothing to do. Once he experimented with fitful enthusiasm to produce a disease-resistant strain of banana but, as soon as the project threatened to tie him down to regular hours of work, he abandoned it.

His chief pleasure lay in the social round. He enjoyed the company of a wide circle of acquaintances, but he made few close friends. He entertained constantly, and was entertained in return; he developed a deep dislike of dining alone and rarely did so. At weekends, he filled Illana's Hall with guests and his invitations were prized not because people found him a diverting host, but on account of the curious beauty of the house which his father had built to the memory of a coloured girl.

He showed no particular wish to marry and, unlike his father, women did not find him an attractive man in spite of his wealth. He was one of the first people on Saint Cecilia to buy a motor car; his black labourers doffed their sweat-stained caps as he passed by and gazed with disbelief at the bucking mechanical monster which transported their Master three times a week to his club in the capital. And if they wondered why it was he did not care to ride into the fields to inspect the work of the estate for himself, no one was ever rash enough to voice his thoughts out loud.

Saint Cecilia's long sleep was broken by the onset of war in 1914. Several hundred black Cecilians volunteered to join the British West India Regiment. In due course some of them were sent to Europe and some to the Middle East where they acquitted themselves well. But when the black soldiers came home four years later it was all seen to have been a mistake, for they brought with them the first incipient challenge to white rule that the island had witnessed since the firing of the Court House at King Charles Bay more than fifty years earlier.

It was not the murderous war itself which had served to open their eyes; it was what they had seen of England. The Mother Country, that paragon among nations whose praises they had been carefully taught to sing in every open air village school, turned out to be very different from what they had been led to expect. To their astonishment, for instance, they discovered that millons of white English men and women lived in slums every inch as rat-infested and disease-ridden as the worst shanty areas of Saint Cecilia's capital; and on the streets of London, at the very heart of the Empire on which the sun never set, they were accosted by brazen white prostitutes openly offering their bodies to black men. It was something that back in their native island would have been beyond the wildest imagining. White people in their own country, they soon came to see, were no more virtuous or admirable – or worthy of respect – than black people in theirs.

But it was a quite different aspect of the English way of life that made the deepest impression: the black soldiers saw for the first time the power that could be wielded by organised labour. They witnessed with their own eyes the miracle of trades unions at work. After that experience, it was certain that change would come to Saint Cecilia.

Predictably, as soon as the war was over, the first demands for a voice in the conduct of their island's affairs came from the returning soldiers; muffled and a little uncertain at first, but growing stronger and more insistent. Their demands touched a secret, responsive chord in every one of their black countrymen.

In his capacity as an adviser to the Governor, Charles Langford noted these developments with concern because he could see, even then, that if left unchecked they would eventually threaten the whole edifice of white rule. There were, after all, more than a hundred black men to every white one on Saint Cecilia. He set his face resolutely against the smallest concession and, when the agitated Governor of the day sought the views of his Privy Councillors, Charles Langford's advice was uncompromising: 'Do not give the niggras an inch,' he said. 'What they are aiming at in the long run is no less than the destruction of white authority.'

It proved to be the general view.

In July 1919, Charles Langford abruptly set aside his concerns about the future of Saint Cecilia and got married. Like his grandfather and his father before him, he left it until late in his life. He was, in fact, fifty-one and his bride was less than half that age. Their marriage was the talk of Cecilian society for many weeks; as a topic of conversation on middle-class verandahs it soon eclipsed the derided ambitions of a handful of disgruntled former soldiers.

Charles's wife was the daughter of the Chief Justice of Saint Cecilia, a member of one of the oldest and most distinguished families on the island. Her own ancestors, like the Langfords, had come from England to the West Indies at the end of the seventeenth century; but hers had not come in shackles like Cleydon. They had been people of substance in their own country, landed gentry, and they had arrived in the Caribbean in some considerable style with gold in their pockets and with their own band of white retainers to offload the crates of silver and fine linen and to build their first high-gabled house. For Charles Langford, the marriage served to complete in his mind the separation between himself and the earlier, uncouth generations of his family. He had succeeded in marrying into exactly that kind of family to which he had always felt he really belonged.

On the day after the wedding, the front page of the Cecilian Daily Times carried a photograph of the couple passing through the arched entrance of the cathedral in the capital, the Governor of the time a few paces behind them as the principal guest.

A UNION OF BEAUTY AND WEALTH read the caption, and beneath it was printed an account of the wedding written in the newspaper's most effusive and ingratiating style.

Ten months later, the same paper carried another item about the Langford family, given similar prominence on the front page. Mrs Charles Langford, it reported, had given birth to a son. There was an affecting picture of mother and child. The Honourable Charles Langford had been pleased to confide to the social reporter the news that his son would be christened Cleydon; it was an old family name, he said. The editor of the paper proffered his warm congratulations to the distinguished couple and wished all good fortune to their infant son.

Tucked away at the bottom right-hand corner of the page, almost lost beneath a bland advertisement for a new tooth powder, there was a three line item of news of a different kind. It was headed: *Ex-Soldiers Present Right to Vote Petition.* According to the brief text, the petition had been intended for the Governor. His Excellency, however, had declined to receive it and the former soldiers had been obliged to leave it at Government House with his chauffeur.

In the years which lay ahead, there would be more than one person who could recall how the newspaper had misjudged the relative importance of the two coincidental events of that distant day.

Part Two

8

Cleydon Langford – the second Cleydon Langford – was born at New Providence estate on the last day of April 1920, a time of the year when the poincianas were in flower and the white walls of Illana's Hall seemed to float on a sea of scarlet petals.

Cleydon's earliest memory was of the soft flow of water in the channels beneath the floor boards of his bedroom. His mother had converted one of the downstairs rooms into a nursery with a smaller room adjacent to it for the use of Thomasina, his black nurse. During the course of the long, hot Caribbean afternoons when he was supposed to rest upon his bed, the door of this room was propped open and the urgent whisper of the stream beneath the house was overlaid by the deeper note of the waterfall in the hall beyond the passage. In later years, all the memories of his early life were to be inextricably bound up with the comforting music of moving water.

He grew up an only child; his mother did not intend to hazard her slim figure by bearing more than one. Although his parents took care to see that he lacked no material advantage money could secure, his strongest emotional tie was to Thomasina, his nurse. He spent nearly all his waking hours in her company and, on most days, he saw his parents only for a short time after breakfast and for an hour or so before his evening meal. His mother liked people and parties, and most of her own evenings were taken up either with the elaborate ritual of dressing to go out to dinner or with preparing to entertain a carefully selected group of friends at home.

On one evening each week, his mother would set aside half an hour to read aloud to him in her bedroom. She would sit in a chair drawn up to her dressing table; he would take his prescribed place on the carpet at her feet. She had once seen in a friend's house a popular Victorian print of such a tableau, and the sentimental nature of the picture had strongly appealed to her.

She read from a cloth bound copy of *Grimm's Fairy Tales* in a slow deliberate manner like a child, and she never once suspected how Cleydon came to detest the cruel, deformed, Germanic world of those hateful stories. From time to time she would stop reading and hold the book down towards him so that he could see the illustrations; because his head was well below the level of her own, she never saw the care he took to avert his eyes from the macabre line drawings.

Precisely at the end of half an hour, no matter where she had reached in the text, she would mark the page and return the book to its place in her dressing table drawer.

'That is all for this week,' she would say. 'I hope you enjoyed the story.'

'Oh, yes,' he would assure her dutifully. 'Thank you for reading to me . . .'

And immediately her attention would turn from her son to the demanding task of deciding which of the evening dresses her maid had earlier laid out for her inspection she would choose to wear that night.

Cleydon would slip tactfully from her room, not needing to be told his time was up.

He might see her again, briefly, when she came to his bed to kiss him goodnight, and on those occasions her perfume would linger like a cloud above his head long after the high-slung Buick, with Barrett the chauffeur at the wheel, had carried her away into the night. His father, who did not believe that men should kiss their sons, always shook him gravely by the hand when the boy was taken to bid him goodnight.

The affection Cleydon craved was provided for him by Thomasina. At night if ever he was frightened by the surge of wind in the branches of the poincianas outside his window, or by the menacing, restless shadows cast upon the wall of his room by the full moon, she was there to comfort him.

Thomasina was a very large, very black woman who always wore a freshly starched white apron and smelt of bay rum and the coconut oil which she used upon her hair. She had six children of her own but, when Cleydon was born and his mother took Thomasina out of the kitchen to be his nurse, she packed them all off to their grandmother's little mud-walled hut in the mountains. She dutifully set aside three days in each year to visit them, but she spoke of them casually as if they were strangers and it was clear that she reserved all her boundless affection for her white charge.

Cleydon said to her once: 'Don't you miss your own children at all?'

'Dey Gran'mother can look after dem well enough, Massa Cleydon,' she replied. 'An' besides, if I was not here who goin' look after you?'

As soon as he was old enough to be taken for walks without demanding to be carried all the way back, he and Thomasina used to slip quietly out of the house each morning in that precious, undefiled interval between first light and sunrise. They would climb the slope of the hill behind the house, following the overgrown, dew-cloaked paths which led deep into the heart of the rain forest that masked the lower valleys of the central mountain range.

Thomasina's father had earned a living as an itinerant charcoal burner and she had been born and brought up in a crude wattle hut balanced on a lonely, precipitous hillside plot of land overlooking the rich fields of New Providence. The family had been very poor, at times almost destitute. As a child, following her father on his endless search for suitable wood on the mountain slopes, Thomasina came to know the common name of every local flower and the precise use to which each medicinal herb could be put. She learnt to tell at a glance what kind of butterfly any one of the hundred different species of caterpillar would eventually become, and – years later – Cleydon never forgot his disappointment on being told by her that those polychrome giants with green and scarlet waistcoats, which lived on the leaves of the frangipani trees, gave rise to nothing more exciting than the familiar, dun-coloured moths that blundered into his bedroom every night through the open window.

'Massa Cleydon,' Thomasina observed in her soft, deep voice when he confessed his disappointment, 'dat is a good lesson to remember. Sometimes in dis life what look pretty don' turn out to have no real value later on, an' what seem ugly can still be good. We-all should learn de colour don' mean a t'ing.'

Once a year, usually in the middle of the dry season when the fierce sun hung day after day in a sky without clouds, the Langford family left New Providence to spend two weeks on one of their smaller properties in a cooler part of the island. Each of these still retained its own Great House, but they were all of them mere dolls' houses by comparison with Illana's Hall, and none could boast a stream which flowed beneath the floorboards of Cleydon's bedroom.

The property in the Blue Mountains, where coffee grew in rich abundance, was more than four thousand feet above sea level. The clapboard estate house clung precariously to the steep slope of a valley and it was propped up at the front by four thin mahogany pillars which gave it a curious, predatory aspect. From the open verandah, the view across the lower foothills of the mountain range to the distant, wrinkled sea took the breath clean away from anyone who had not seen it before. It was cold up there at nights and, when daylight faded, the family closed the jalousie windows and lit a pine log fire in the living room. The servants padded about unhappily with blankets thrown over their shoulders; after dinner, one of the shivering maids placed stone hot water bottles in all the beds to take the edge off the unaccustomed chill.

Each morning when Cleydon leapt out of bed, he would find the house wrapped in a blanket of mist; the thin, disembodied voices of the labourers gathering for work in the valley below drifted up to him through the mist like echoes from another world. The mist clung to the dripping branches of the silk cotton trees around the house and swirled about the pillars which supported the verandah; in the stillness that flowed back after the black men and women had scattered to their various tasks in the coffee fields, the silence of the valley was disturbed only by the sad, sweet notes of the *siffleurs montagnes*.

The rising sun dispersed the mist. At one moment the house would be wrapped in a damp grey blanket; then, without warning, a golden shaft of light would pierce the gloom and instantly the mist would be drawn up the side of the mountain and out of sight. Cleydon used to sit patiently on the verandah every morning to witness the miracle take place, shivering violently at first in his thin cotton pyjamas, then exulting in the splendid, familiar warmth of the sun. The swift transformation never lost its charm for him; it was one of the many things – like the matchless intensity of the blue of the empty sky behind them – that he came to love about those mountains.

In the isolated branches of the valleys far below, where the probing fingers of sunlight did not reach until later in the morning, wisps of cloud still hovered persistently over the trees long after the house had been bathed in light. Cleydon used to watch the struggle of the mist to stay alive as it retreated before the inexorable advance of the sunlight up the valleys, until the last pale shadow had been consumed.

On fine evenings, Charles Langford would take his son with him on a walk through the fields of coffee which surrounded the stilt-legged house, and sometimes they pressed on into the trackless forest beyond the borders of their land. On the way they met the gangs of labourers trudging back in the soft evening light to their huts on the slopes of the valley below. As their employer approached, they scuttled to the side of the path and waited respectfully, caps in hands, for him to pass by.

'Evenin' baas,' they chorused. 'Evenin' young Massa.' And Charles Langford would return their greetings and inquire perfunctorily about the state of their health. He adopted a stern tone of voice whenever he spoke to his black employees, a rare occurrence at the best of times, 'just to make sure that they don't forget who's who,' as he put it. And if the dutiful smiles of his labourers were a little wider than was natural, and were not reflected in their tired eyes, he never appeared to notice.

On one occasion an English friend of the family, who was spending a few days with them in the mountains, accompanied his host on one of those evening walks through the well-groomed fields of coffee. They encountered a little group of labourers on the path and the usual greetings were exchanged. When the black men and women had passed out of earshot, the friend wondered aloud about the quality of their lives. Might they not, one day, seek to change the order of things by asking for a voice in the conduct of their own affairs? he mused. Would they always passively accept the state of poverty in which they lived?

The friend had meant no harm, but Charles Langford was affronted. The thought that any one of those ragged labourers might not be content with things as they were had never occurred to him; the very idea was offensive. He halted in mid-stride on the path ahead. He raised his mahoe walking stick dramatically into the air and pointed with it in the general direction of the unhappy Negro republic of Haiti.

'Do you have any idea at all of what goes on over there, less than three hundred miles from where we stand?' he demanded to know. 'Don't you realise what happens when black men are given power to govern themselves? No one in his right mind would want to inflict that kind of self-punishment upon these ignorant people. They are perfectly content as they are, and we must see to it that no trouble-makers are allowed to suggest otherwise to them.'

His voice had risen sharply as he spoke and Cleydon, who was with them, knew that his father was very angry. The family friend was wise enough not to pursue the subject, lest it be imagined by his host that he might condone the trouble-makers or, worse, be numbered among them himself; and so they walked on through the hushed valley in silence, each of them cocooned in the cloak of his separate thoughts.

For Cleydon's part, he did not for one moment imagine that his father might be wrong; it seemed to him at the time only in the nature of things as he knew them that white men should command and black men should obey.

The Langford family owned another satellite estate which Cleydon loved to visit, a place where everything was in the sharpest possible contrast to the property in the mountains. It was a small banana plantation which lay in a fertile crescent of land along the north-eastern shore of the island. It had been one of those bankrupt properties shrewdly bought up by Jonas Langford for a few hundred pounds in the bad times that had followed the emancipation of the slaves in 1838. Many years later, Charles Langford's attorney had rooted out the sugar cane with which it had been planted for more than a hundred years, and he had replaced that crop with trim fields of more profitable bananas.

When Cleydon was a boy, the gaunt brick chimney which once served the sugar factory still kept silent watch over the land within sight of the sea. Only the reptilian roots of a giant banyan tree, which bound together the crumbling fabric of the ruined building at its base, prevented its long delayed collapse.

The coastline of the estate was a succession of towering

limestone cliffs, broken at just one place where the restless sea had searched out some ancient weakness in the pitted rock and carved into it a perfect horseshoe cove.

The mouth of the little bay was scarcely thirty feet across and the lime green water within it was entirely protected from all but the roughest sea outside. The beach was a steep arc of coral sand, bounded above high water mark by a crescent of coconut palms. In a rocky depression beyond the beach there was a freshwater pond where hastate saffron lilies pierced the reflection of the sky. On the green slope between the pond and the beach, Jonas Langford had once planted a grove of casuarina trees and the sand beneath them was carpeted with their delicate fallen needles.

The clapboard estate house – a Great House in name only – stood on the cliffs at the mouth of the bay. In stormy weather, when the waves which drove in from the south-east exploded against the limestone shore, broad sheets of spray were carried up the face of the cliffs and clear over the shingle roof of the house. Cleydon used to crawl as close as he dared to the edge of the cliffs to watch the white-capped rollers gather strength for their final assault upon the land. The earth shook beneath him, there was a roar like thunder in his ears and the sun crusted the salt thick along his naked back.

He was to retain one childhood memory of the place which he treasured above all others. He was eight years old at the time and he was walking the short length of the beach one morning at sunrise. He was alone, for even Thomasina had declined his invitation to be up and about at that hour. There had been a storm the previous day, but the wind had blown itself out overnight and beyond the mouth of the little bay the sea stretched away towards the taut horizon like a sheet of beaten silver. A disordered fleet of fishing canoes passed across the mouth of the bay, their passage briefly marked by the vanishing scars of their separate wakes. On the crisp, damp surface of the sand, washed clean by the night's high tide, the resident colony of ghost crabs had inscribed an intricate pattern of interwoven tracks. The iodine scent of sergasso weed was heavy on the air.

All along the line of the high water, little windrows of empty shells had been cast up and then abandoned by the retreating tide. They were mostly common species, already represented in the collection stored with such care in his room back at Illana's Hall, but as he approached the end of the beach where the sand gave place abruptly to the steep limestone rock, he caught sight of the elliptic outline of a Lion's Paw scallop, half screened by a sheet of torquoise sea lettuce tossed by chance upon it by the waves.

He had already learnt enough about shells to recognise this as a rare species; the only traces of its kind he had previously discovered were a few abraded fragments carried up from deep water by the heavy ground swell that follows a storm. This specimen, however, was complete, without a single blemish, the double valves gaping wide to reveal the dead creature still within them.

The scallop was about the size of a tea plate, heavily ribbed on the outside of both valves. It was coloured a rich maroon, shading at the umbones into palest amber, and it seemed to him at first a thing of such delicate beauty that he was half afraid to lift it from its bed on the sand in case it somehow crumbled in his grasp; but he found that it was stoutly made. With the aid of a sharpened twig, he washed away the soft parts at the water's edge. As the valves gaped wide, he saw that the interior of the shell was on fire with colour. In the centre of each valve there was a great burst of brilliant orange laced by pinks and mauves and the softest trace of green; it was, he realised, a faithful reflection of the splendour of a West Indian sunset.

The discovery of the scallop spurred his interest in shells. Back at Illana's Hall, cardboard shoe boxes came in time to fill the cupboards of his room and to overflow on to the floor beside his bed. For his ninth birthday present, he chose to ask for a double-fronted mahogany cabinet fitted with sliding drawers. It took one of the estate carpenters six weeks to make and it was a thing of beauty in itself. It was delivered to the house while he sat at breakfast on the morning of his birthday. He never forgot the intense happiness of the days that followed, as he transferred his shells from their over-crowded cardboard quarters to the splendid setting of the new cabinet. When it was done, he invited his parents to view the collection in its new home; they promised to set aside half an hour after tea that day to do so. Friends came in the afternoon to visit them, however, and the appointment was never kept. It was left to Thomasina to admire the artful way in which he had arranged his limpets and his polished cowries and to marvel with him over the beauty of the Lion's Paw scallop which he had displayed in isolated glory upon a bed of cotton wool.

'Don' fuss you'self' cause Massa an' Mistress too busy to see dem,' Thomasina comforted him at the end of the day. 'I admire dem an' you admire dem, an' dat should be sufficient.'

And, in the event, Cleydon found it so.

During Cleydon's childhood, New Providence employed about six hundred labourers at crop time, most of whom worked either in the cane fields or upon the floor of the sugar factory. More than half of these men and women, however, were laid off after the new cane had been planted, when the only work to be done was weeding between the rows and simple maintenance in the factory. For those labourers who owned a plot of land in the mountains, this annual holiday without pay was no great hardship because it gave them the time they needed to cultivate their own soil. They planted yams and sweet potatoes and gathered ackees and breadfruit from the trees which stood around their huts, and on the whole they were content.

Those who had no land of their own, however, were obliged to live in barrack accommodation provided by the estate. At New Providence, the Barracks was a narrow, clapboard building raised several feet above the marshy ground on which it stood by arthritic wooden pillars. When the rains arrived in June, the low-lying land around the building was soon flooded and, on bad days, the sullen brown water climbed the frail supports and lapped close against the underside of the open, pitch pine floors. Every evening at dusk, a black cloud of mosquitoes rose in obedience to some silent insect signal from the nearby swamps and fell upon the people of the Barracks.

The ugly structure was divided internally by plywood partitions and just one of the square wooden boxes formed in this way was allocated to each family that lived there. The partitions rose only seven feet from the floor: at night the occupants of those bleak rooms lay on beds of coarse sacking and listened unwillingly to the muffled medley of children crying and of their parents seeking what pleasure they could find in each other's tired bodies.

Those labourers who, by some unexpected stroke of good fortune, were able later to escape the crowded misery of the Barracks to a hut of their own, invariably looked back upon those earlier times with a bitterness and resentment which the passage of the years never quite erased from their minds.

Cleydon was never permitted to play with the black children of the Barracks when he was a boy and, as he grew older, his father felt it necessary to explain the reason why.

'We have to think ahead to when you grow up,' he said. 'The time will come when New Providence and the other properties we hold will pass to you. You will be one of the largest landowners on this island; you will have a position to maintain and people will look to you to set an example in many things.'

He searched for words to explain the truth as he saw it.

'The truth is that God has set a distance between us, the white Masters, and them, the black servants. No doubt we have a duty to be fair to them, but they are not like us and they never will be. They are a shiftless and untrustworthy race, and we must see to it that the gulf that separates us now remains as wide as ever in the years ahead. We must keep our distance to hold on to our authority. Familiarity breeds contempt; and that is why you cannot play with their children.'

It was the longest speech Cleydon had ever heard him deliver. Where his son was concerned, he was usually a man of few words. On this occasion they were sitting together on the verandah of Illana's Hall; it was evening and on the slopes of the mountains behind them, the Caribbean night was gathering itself to fall upon their land all in one piece like a shutter. Charles Langford looked out over the darkening fields of cane towards the distant sea; he had not finished.

'This island belongs to us, not to them,' he said. 'They are here because we brought them from Africa to work for us, that is all. God gave us a trust in this matter and we must not betray it.'

Cleydon believed every word; and as a consequence he never thought to question why it was he grew up at New Providence without the companionship of boys his own age. Clearly, if God himself had decided that black men should remain the servants of white men, then friendship between them was impossible. It was common sense when you looked at it like that, he thought, but he was discomforted by the problem of how he ought to apply all this to Thomasina who was very black indeed but who, at the same time, was closer to him than any other human being.

When Cleydon was nine years old, a private tutor was engaged for him. The man was a retired English schoolmaster who lived with the Langfords at Illana's Hall until the boy was twelve and old enough to be sent to boarding school.

The tutor was a silent, withdrawn individual whose pale personality made little impression on his pupil. Years later, Cleydon learnt that as a young man he had suffered some unbearable disappointment from which he had never successfully recovered. From time to time, he would interrupt the course of his lessons to observe in his sepulchral voice: 'Life is abominably cruel. If you give it the smallest opportunity, it will strike you down. Always you must be on your guard against the spitefulness of fate. That is a far more important lesson to learn than any you will discover in your text books.'

On his return voyage to England at the end of his three years in Saint Cecilia, the man threw himself from the deck of his ship and was drowned.

The unfortunate tutor's departure was followed by Cleydon's own despatch to boarding school. The school was set high in the mountains at the very centre of Saint Cecilia. The squat, unprepossessing buildings were shaped from massive limestone blocks quarried from the face of a nearby cliff. The buildings lay in a broad ellipse about a central playing field. With the passage of time, a coat of grey-green lichen had worked its way across the white stone walls until, from a distance, they seemed to melt into the background of the rain forest behind them and so to disappear from view.

Inside the buildings, generations of boys had left all the usual destructive signs of their passage and, at night in the open dormitory, Cleydon used to lie on his canvas cot and listen to the relentless ticking of the death watch beetles at work on the old beams and joists of the attic above his head. The nights were cold and cheerless at that school and, unlike the stilt-legged house among the coffee fields of the Blue Mountains, no fires were permitted to temper the chill of the mist which settled over the place after sunset.

The school had been established at the beginning of the eighteenth century by the Anglican Church. In the words of its Charter, its purpose was to provide an education for the sons of gentlemen resident in the island of Saint Cecilia. Only after the end of the First World War did the Governors reluctantly concede that it might be politic to offer one scholarship a year to a black boy – though, of course, by no exercise of the imagination could the fathers of such pupils be described as gentlemen.

Nevertheless, from that time, in the annual photograph of the school population traditionally taken with the grim

123

facade of the assembly hall in the background, there would be five or six black faces, scattered like raisins in a cake, among the sea of white ones.

The boys who won this scholarship were invariably boys of outstanding ability and ambition; but their presence was deeply resented by the great majority of the white boys, who naturally reflected their parents' opinions. Whatever advantage attendance at that school gave to the black scholars later in their lives, it was hard earned, and it etched on their souls scars which they carried with them for the rest of their days.

They were bullied unmercifully. At meals in the dining hall, they were obliged to eat by themselves in a corner screened from the rest by a broad wooden pillar. In the dormitories, beds were rearranged to create a sanitary cordon between their cots and those of the other boys. In the classrooms, they were consigned to the back row. At the end of each day, they were forced to wait for the use of the showers until all the white boys had bathed and changed.

The scholars accepted their lot as something that had to be stoically endured, just as their ancestors had endured the pain and indignity of slavery and yet survived. They arrived at the age of twelve with the certain knowledge that their lives for the next six years would be full of difficulty; but they also knew that at the end of that time they would at least be assured of a comfortable place in the junior ranks of the island's Civil Service; and, for the very cleverest, there was always the remote chance of winning another scholarship to an English university.

Beneath the air of weary resignation which they all soon came to adopt, however, a bitter resentment simmered and, just occasionally, boiled over into a sudden, uncontrollable eruption of fury. Then, one of the black boys, goaded beyond endurance, bravely turned on his tormentors only to be felled by a rain of kicks and cuffs delivered by half a dozen white boys who had been waiting impatiently on the sidelines for just such a desperate explosion of rage.

9

The scholarship winner the year Cleydon arrived to take his place in the first form was a tall, thin-faced boy called Lampit with a skin so black that even the darkest of the school servants seemed almost pale by comparison. Many – perhaps most – Cecilians carried in their veins some admixture of white blood, unmistakable evidence of the slave owners' practice of coupling with their black chattels; but no one could doubt that Lampit was pure African.

To add to the handicap of his colour, the boy was afflicted in that first year with a nervous stammer which could render him incoherent for several minutes at a time. Predictably, this combination of misfortunes led to a merciless harassment which never really abated throughout his subsequent years at the school, even after he had conquered his stammer by a brave effort of will.

He took it all in silence; he accepted the constant humiliations with a strange, defiant dignity. It did not in any way deter his tormenters, but Cleydon used to have the curious feeling that although their blows undoubtedly hurt his body they could not reach his spirit. No one ever saw him cry.

From the very first day of term, it was clear that Lampit was the cleverest boy in Cleydon's class, and during the following six years he worked harder than anyone else and outdistanced them all. He sat at his desk in the furthest corner of the classroom, dressed in his shabby, ill-fitting khaki clothes which were the best his mother could afford, his black head bent over his books, his mind concentrated on his work, apparently unaware of the hostile presence of the other boys around him. Those long hours in the classroom, so deadly tedious for everyone else, were for him the only tolerable part of the school day. There at least he was safe from the harassment which faced him every afternoon when lessons came to an end, and there he could get on with the task of preparing himself for the great role he was already convinced that destiny had reserved for him after he left school.

Because he quickly discovered, as did all the black boys, that his appearance on the cricket or football field signalled a concerted attack by his enemies, he avoided games and spent the time instead with his books. By the end of his first term, he was placed third overall in the class, an astonishing, unprecedented achievement for a scholarship boy who had been confronted by subjects like algebra and Latin which were not taught at all in his previous school. By the time the year drew to its close, Lampit's name had appeared at the top of the class list and it remained there for the rest of his time at school.

For the boys who tormented him so relentlessly day after day, the realisation that a black boy had proved himself cleverer than all his white contemporaries was painful to accept; though they found a hundred excuses for it, the immediate result was to harden their determination to make Lampit's life more difficult than ever before.

Lampit and Cleydon Langford spent all six years of their schooling in the same classes. They were promoted together, though Lampit's name always appeared well above Cleydon's on the list posted on the common room notice board at the start of each September term. They progressed side by side, and so Cleydon was an ever-present witness to what the black boy had to endure in the course of those six long years.

Cleydon took no part himself in the bullying of Lampit; but looking back on it all years later he acknowledged that he had made no serious effort to restrain it. He knew that any attempt by him and the handful of other boys who disliked it would have been futile; no doubt they would have succeeded only in attracting some of the same treatment themselves. In addition to this, the truth was that he, too, felt that a black boy had no right to be at that school.

Nevertheless, occasionally when the opportunity arose, Cleydon tried to show Lampit that he could consider him, if not a friend, at least something less than an enemy; but the black boy steadfastly rejected any kind of overture with the same distant, cold-eyed stare which he turned upon the boys who beat him. Cleydon was white and, not surprisingly, in Lampit's eyes all white boys were hostile. He was prepared to admit no exceptions and, when Cleydon thought about it, he could scarcely blame him.

Only twice in all his years at school did that iron mask of self-control slip far enough for Lampit to reveal any true emotion. On the first occasion, the school day had just ended and Cleydon's class was clattering down the worn wooden staircase which led to the cobbled courtyard and the playing fields beyond it. Lampit was directly in front of him. He had reached the third step from the bottom when one of the white boys deliberately thrust out a foot and tripped him. Lampit was carrying a loose bundle of books and he fell heavily down the stairs, striking his head against the bannister and cutting his lip on the bottom step. The books went flying from his grasp and were scattered over the cobbles at the base of the stairs. One of them fell directly in the path of the boy who had tripped him; he kicked it as hard as he could across the yard. Then he strode off contemptuously towards the cricket field, where the other boys were already squabbling among themselves about whose turn it was to bat first.

The book landed beside Cleydon. He picked it up and walked back to where the black boy was sitting on the cobbled apron; he looked dazed and shaken, but defiant still. A thin stream of blood was running from the corner of his mouth to the point of his chin. Against the blue-blackness of his skin it was scarcely visible, but bright scarlet drops fell upon the pale cover of the English note book he held in his hands. The class had been doing *The Merchant of Venice* as a set book that term; the quotation sprang unbidden to Cleydon's mind:

'If you prick us, do we not bleed? . . . If you poison us, do we not die? . . . And if you wrong us, shall we not revenge?'

He looked at the book he had picked out of the dust. He noticed at once that it was not one of the school text books. The title was printed in large gold letters across the top of the jacket: *Heroes of the Negro Race*, it read. Directly beneath the title was an extravagantly coloured painting of Chaka, the great Zulu king, a leopard-skin cape flung carelessly across his shoulders, in his leather headband a long blue feather, that symbol of kingship that only he could wear. About him stood a bodyguard of coal black warriors, the bright blades of their assegais reflecting the harsh African sunlight, and beyond them were the impis, drawn up in massed formation. The men held themselves with haughty grace; they looked like a people who recognised no master but their own king. Cleydon noticed that there were no white men in the picture.

He handed the book back to Lampit. The boy took it without a word and there was an expression in his eyes of such intense hatred that for a moment Cleydon wondered whether Lampit had mistakenly thought that he was the boy who had tripped him. As if he had read Cleydon's thoughts, Lampit said in his deep, quiet voice: 'I know it was not you. But no matter; when the time comes you all goin' stan' at the same bar of judgement.'

Cleydon could think of no apt reply to that, so he left him sitting there in the dust, the blood still dripping from his injured lip; and in the years which lay ahead, he never forgot the look in the boy's dark, accusing eyes.

Lampit and Cleydon spent their last two years at school together in the sixth form, working in their different ways for their Higher Certificates. Lampit was taking four subjects;

Cleydon, with less ability and less ambition, only two. In the more relaxed atmosphere at the top of the school they came to know each other better. The worst of the bullies had left at the end of the previous year. Most of the sixth formers were appointed prefects; Cleydon was one himself. But Lampit held no position in the school except that which he had won by his own efforts in the classroom.

During the course of their last year, there was talk that Lampit stood a chance of winning the Rhodes Scholarship to Oxford and, because this was a distinction never achieved by a boy from that school, the Headmaster suddenly began to display an interest in him which he had not shown before. No doubt he regretted that if one of his boys was going to win the scholarship it should not be a white one, but a black recipient was better than none at all, for there was great prestige attached to the award established, so ironically in this case, by the arch-advocate of white dominion in Africa.

In May 1937, the school was unexpectedly granted a holiday in the middle of the week to mark the coronation of the new king in London. For Cleydon it meant the arrival of Barrett in the Buick to drive him back to New Providence and the prospect of a day spent lazing on the beach or shooting teal from his dinghy on the river. For Lampit, on the other hand, the unexpected holiday presented a problem: his scholarship to the school only just met the anticipated expenses of each term, and his mother was forced to calculate down to the last penny exactly how the small grant could best be spent. Her reckoning had to include the cost of his bus fare to and from the capital, where they lived, at the beginning and end of each term, but it did not take into account unscheduled holidays when the school was closed and all boarders were expected to return to their homes. Lampit's problem was that he had no money to pay his bus fare home on this occasion in the middle of the term.

There were, of course, many other boys whose homes were in the capital and whose parents would be sending cars to fetch them. But Lampit, whose family did not even own a bicycle, could not bring himself to ask one of them for a lift, and no one offered to take him with them.

Cleydon could never remember just how he became aware of Lampit's dilemma, but on the afternoon prior to the holiday, without giving any real thought to the implications of what he was doing, he invited the boy to come back to New Providence with him.

Lampit's immediate reaction was flatly to reject the invitation; he did not even consider it necessary to invent an excuse.

'I don't have to accept charity from you or from anyone else,' he said stiffly. 'If I have to, I can walk home.'

But both of them knew that this was impossible; the capital was seventy miles away. Then their Housemaster made it clear that no one would be allowed to remain at the school during the holiday; the staff, too, intended to have a day off. With deep reluctance, Lampit finally agreed to go to New Providence with Cleydon.

'But you don't have to take me into your house,' he announced defiantly. 'You can leave me in the servants' quarters – and I know you must have plenty of those.'

Cleydon let the jibe pass. With some trepidation he sought the use of the Housemaster's telephone to tell his parents what he had done. The line to New Providence was bad and at first he could not get his father to understand that the boy he intended to bring back with him as his guest for the holiday was black. When Charles Langford finally grasped what his son was trying to say, there was a shocked silence; the telephone crackled and spat in Cleydon's ear and, for a moment, Cleydon thought that his father had hung up. Then, in that soft, resonant voice which Charles Langford always used when he was trying to curb his swift temper, Cleydon heard him say: 'If you wanted to bring a friend, for God's sake why didn't you invite someone whose parents we know like you always do?'

Cleydon tried to explain the circumstances, that in any event it would only be for one night, but partly because the line was growing worse and partly because he did not want a black boy as a guest in his house, his father pretended that he could not hear.

Up to that moment, Cleydon could quite easily have been persuaded to drop the whole idea; he already regretted the impulsive invitation: he had been foolish. His father's attitude angered him, however. He was suddenly determined that Lampit should come to New Providence with him and he said so.

'Well, all right,' his father said at last, his voice rising above the interference on the line, 'but don't expect your mother and me to eat with him. We'll arrange for you two to have your meals an hour earlier. You can eat in the old nursery. God only knows what the servants will think,' he added furiously.

Cleydon said goodbye and hung up.

Barrett arrived with the Buick the following afternoon as the school day ended. At once the difficulties began. Lampit refused to sit in the back of the car with Cleydon; he did not wish to be seen lording it in that way as white people did. At the same time, Cleydon could tell that Barrett, with that curious contempt which many Negroes felt for members of their own race, was outraged that he should be driving a black boy to stay at Illana's Hall as a guest.

Lampit was uncompromising. Eventually they all sat together uncomfortably on the front seat, Lampit sandwiched in the middle, silent, brooding and, so it seemed, determined to be as awkward as possible.

Barrett's disapproval was evident in the set line of his jaw. Usually, on the long journey back to New Providence at the end of each term, he would bring Cleydon up to date with all the latest gossip of the estate; and, if Cleydon was very persuasive, he would disregard his employer's stern orders and allow the boy to take the wheel of the big car on a deserted stretch of the road beyond the mountains.

On this occasion, however, he said nothing at all and kept his eyes firmly fixed on the road ahead. Cleydon was furious with him and equally angry now with himself for having invited Lampit to Illana's Hall in the first place.

They turned off the main road at last and drove up the long, palm-flanked avenue which led between the fields of cane to the house. The white walls came into view beyond a cluster of flowering poincianas; the Buick passed over a broad carpet of scarlet blossom. Cleydon looked sideways at Lampit and could tell at once that the extravagant beauty of the Hall and its setting had served only to arouse the boy's hostility. He took one long look at the front of the house with its double flight of elegant marble steps and said: 'When they say that some people built up their fortunes on the backs of black slaves, it is this that they have in mind.'

Above the drumming of the tyres on the gravelled fore-court, Cleydon could hear Barrett's swift intake of breath at this unprecedented impertinence on the part of a black boy; one, moreover, who was going to be privileged to eat and sleep in the Great House. And Cleydon knew for certain then that, no matter how he might struggle to avert it, the holiday was going to be a disaster.

He introduced Lampit to his mother and father; Lampit averted his eyes, said nothing and, so it seemed to Cleydon, shook their extended hands with the greatest distaste. Had he been white, his behaviour might have been put down to shyness, but Lampit was not shy. He was gauche and a little unsure of himself in such company, in spite of his iron determination to be neither impressed nor intimidated by Cleydon's parents or by the style in which they lived, but he was not shy. It was simply that he had filed all white people together in the same drawer of his mind and he despised them. Somehow, Cleydon had imagined that once removed from the environment of the school he hated with such good reason, his attitude would change; he was quite wrong.

On the following day, Cleydon took Lampit with him on a tour of the estate, in a half-hearted attempt to entertain his guest by showing him over the sugar factory and the workshops which serviced and repaired the heavy trucks. But Lampit was interested in none of these things; what he really wanted was an opportunity to speak to the labourers. Without a word, he deserted Cleydon's guided tour and sought them out in the fields, asking them how much they earned and how many hours a week they were obliged to work for their pay. They were being exploited, he promptly informed them; they should band together to protect themselves; they should create their own trade union.

When at last Cleydon persuaded Lampit to return to the Hall for lunch, the black boy immediately put the same questions to Rollins the butler, who had been with the Langford family for more than thirty years. The dignified old man, immaculate as always in his starched white jacket with its polished metal buttons, pretended not to hear him and took prudent refuge in the warren of passages leading off his pantry. His dilemma was painful to witness; there had never been a black guest at Illana's Hall before, and all his training and experience had not prepared him to cope with such an unsettling phenomenon.

Lampit and Cleydon were served their meals alone in the old nursery, on the transparent pretext that Cleydon's parents were accustomed to take their own meals at a different hour. Lampit saw through this at once, of course, and said so without the slightest hesitation.

'I see your mother and father don't want to eat with me because I am black,' he announced. Cleydon made no attempt to reply, because he knew that it was true. They ate alone in silence.

The long day drew to its close and the two boys prepared to return to school the way they had come, on the front seat of the Buick. Lampit took leave of Cleydon's parents with a degree of insolence that snatched Cleydon's breath away. He watched his father go red in the face and saw his fingers tighten involuntarily about the handle of his walking stick; then they were gone, with Barrett once again silent and disapproving at the wheel of the big car.

Two days later, Cleydon found a terse note from his father waiting for him in the school letter rack.

'My dear boy,' it read, 'I do not think it necessary for me or your mother to say what we thought of the behaviour of the black boy you brought with you to New Providence for the holiday.

'I really do not understand the circumstances which prompted you to bring him here and do not wish to. However, I hope that some good may come of it in that you will now have seen for yourself what I have always maintained: these people cannot be put in the same box as ourselves. Because we brought them here from their African jungle we have a duty to look after them, but this duty must be in the context of Master to servant – benevolent Master, but respectful servant. You will recall that I have said it before. That little nigger has some painful lessons to learn.'

A few months after Lampit's unfortunate visit to New Providence, the long pent-up resentment of the black population at a level of wages which chained most of them to a miserable, hopeless existence, erupted at last in a violent series of strikes and riots all over the island. The riots were spontaneous expressions of rage and frustration, and they were plainly directed against white landowners like the Langfords. They paralysed the life of the island and, for the first time since the uprising at King Charles Bay seventy years before, a little shudder of fear passed through the white population.

The troubles quickly threw up leaders, for the most part brave opportunists who knew instinctively that it might just be possible to ride the wave of popular discontent to reach positions of influence which were otherwise closed to them.

134

For the first time the cry from the streets was not only for more bread but for the vote and for self-government.

The rioters set fire to buildings, looted shops and clashed inevitably with the police. And, just as inevitably, the police on the command of their white officers opened fire with their old Lee-Enfield rifles. Black men and women fell in the streets and the resident British garrison was called in by the Governor to restore order. The Colonial Office in London was provoked into setting up a Commission of Inquiry to discover why the riots had occurred in the first place, and for a while after that it seemed to many Cecilians that life had returned to normal; but the calm that followed was deceptive and, although not one of the white families would have guessed it at the time, nothing was ever really going to be the same.

At New Providence the Langfords were lucky. Unlike several of their neighbours, they had little trouble. A few of the younger workers withheld their labour in the cane fields and an unexplained fire destroyed one of the overseer's houses and damaged a corner of the sugar factory, but when the self-appointed leaders of the rioters arrived from the capital to hold a public meeting on his land, Charles Langford instructed his attorney that any of his employees seen within half a mile of the meeting would lose his job next morning. As a result of this threat, the meeting was sparsely attended and the speakers soon moved on to more promising venues.

At Cleydon's school, the white boys reflected the severe views of their parents: the niggers were getting above themselves again and an example should be made of their leaders. It was time they were given another lesson like the one taught on the hanging boom at King Charles Bay in 1865.

Lampit, on the other hand, made no attempt to hide his satisfaction or his passionate desire – had it been possible – to join the rioters on the streets.

135

Then, one stifling afternoon later in 1938, they heard that there had been a violent clash between police and demonstrators on an estate in the western quarter of the island. The police had opened fire and among those who fell was a pregnant woman. The story spread swiftly through the school and was embroidered and exaggerated as it passed from one boy to another: the police bullet had ripped open the woman's abdomen and the living foetus had fallen from her body to the ground. There was an initial moment of shocked revulsion, then everyone seemed to be agreed: this was the only way to treat the rioters, the only kind of message black trouble-makers understood.

Pre-occupied with his own thoughts about the incident, Cleydon had completely forgotten Lampit when at the end of the day they found themselves by chance alone in the sixth form classroom. Cleydon was packing up his books; Lampit left his own place at the back of the room and sat down uninvited in the empty seat beside him. It was a thing Cleydon had never known him to do in all the years they had been together at that school.

Lampit wanted to talk.

'I hear you and the others discussing the shooting,' he began, unable to keep the excitement from his voice, 'but I wonder if you all have any real idea of what it means?'

And, without waiting for Cleydon's reply, Lampit proceeded to tell him.

'It means this island has woken up,' he said. 'It means at last black people are beginning to demand what is owed to them.'

There had been rain in the mountains earlier that day and the evening was cool and overcast, but Cleydon noticed that all along Lampit's upper lip little beads of sweat were standing out against the skin.

'The bullet that ripped open that black woman's belly,' he continued, 'that bullet is going to bring freedom to all Cecilians that look like me. We have our own martyrs now.'

He paused to choose his words with care. 'You have seen what I have suffered at this school. Well, mark this, Langford: my children will never suffer like me; when their turn comes, this will be a black school.'

In his evident excitement, he began to lapse into the vernacular of the alley where he was born. 'Ah goin' tell yuh again what dis whole t'ing mean, Langford. It mean Massa day done.'

Cleydon looked up at him and saw that the boy was smiling, his even teeth very white against the velvet blackness of his skin. Cleydon had never seen him smile before; it transformed his thin face.

'Massa day done,' he repeated slowly, savouring the words as he spoke them. 'We goin' t'row out de white man.'

Cleydon had no wish to argue with him; while he was in that curious, truculent mood it would plainly be a waste of time. Nevertheless, he felt that Lampit needed to be reminded of certain truths.

'You are forgetting something,' he said mildly. 'Everybody knows that black people couldn't run this country on their own; look at what goes on in Haiti right next door to us. Life on this island is good as it is; only trouble-makers want to change it.'

At once Cleydon realised that he would have been wiser to have ignored the boy. Lampit sprang out of his seat, his dark eyes wild with fury. 'Life is good for you, yes,' he hissed, 'but not for us. You-all never intend to treat black people like human beings. You bring us here as slaves, but dis islan' belong to us now; is our sweat an' blood dat mek de soil fertile an' produce de wealth.'

He paused to wipe the sweat from his own temples. 'You-all mus' leave,' he repeated. 'It may tek time to get rid of you; maybe not dis year nor de next; but it goin' happen in my lifetime . . .' He took a deep breath: 'Ah goin' live to see dis islan' become a black man's paradise.'

His voice had risen as he spoke until at the end he was

almost shouting; his expression was ecstatic, like that of a man who has seen a vision.

'A black man's paradise . . .' he repeated, his gaze focussed on the fertile plains of the white-owned estates which he could see through the open window of the classroom, spread out between the base of the mountain range and the distant sea.

He looked round slowly, as if seeing Cleydon for the first time; with a huge effort of will, he brought his emotions back under control.

'I am sorry for you, Langford,' he said quietly, 'because your family owns much property; but it is like I say: Massa day is done.'

As it turned out, this was the last conversation Cleydon was to have with Lampit at that school; they both left two months later at the end of the academic year as soon as they had taken their Higher Certificate examinations. In January 1939, it was announced, just as many people had predicted, that Lampit had won the Rhodes Scholarship to Oxford; his unsmiling photograph appeared on an inside page of the daily newspaper. In the meantime, Cleydon prepared himself to leave for another, lesser English university where, for no particular reason, he intended to read history for three years. Unlike Lampit, he was not going because he had won a place through hard work and natural ability, but simply because his father thought it would be a good idea and he could afford to pay for it all. Cleydon himself did not think that a degree in history would prove to be of much help when the time eventually arrived for him to take over the Langford estates, but that was still a distant prospect. He decided that his aim should be to enjoy his three years in England as much as he possibly could and not to be unduly hampered by any need to apply himself to his studies.

He met Lampit again purely by chance about a month before he was due to leave for England. They collided with each other on the crowded main street of the capital where both had chosen the same day to buy the thick, unfamiliar clothing with which they intended to confront the English climate. Cleydon stopped briefly to congratulate Lampit on winning his scholarship. Lampit brushed aside the words with an impatient wave of his hand; then, as if it were something he had planned long before, he said: 'You took me to your house once; now that you are here, I want you to see mine.

Immediately Cleydon reached for the first excuse that came to mind, for he had no wish to become involved with Lampit in any way again; but Lampit was insistent. Reluctantly, Cleydon agreed.

Lampit led him away from the busy shops with their opulent, American-inspired window displays and the double row of expensive cars parked outside – among them, Cleydon's much loved drop-head Alvis which had been a school leaving present from his parents. Five minutes later, they arrived in a very different part of the city.

Like everyone else, Cleydon knew that the capital had its slums, but he had never been driven by curiosity to seek them out. The streets they followed became progressively more filthy and neglected the further they moved away from the centre; soon they were scarcely distinguishable from open sewers. Foul smelling streams of blue-black water crept sluggishly down them towards the harbour. Decaying refuse of every description lay scattered along the sides of the roads; bands of half-wild pigs and starving, desperate dogs rooted together in the rubbish and challenged each other for whatever putrid scraps of food it contained. The little rivers of filth steamed in the fierce heat of the morning sun and the acrid stench of human excrement hung over all. They stopped for a moment before crossing the road and at once a dark cloud of bluebottles rose from the ground in front of Cleydon and sought to settle on his face.

It took him several minutes fully to realise that it was here Lampit lived.

The houses on either side of the road down which they now walked were frail matchboxes perched upon rickety stilts that raised them some distance above the level of the soil. They were roofed with rusting sheets of corrugated iron and, wherever their unpainted clapboard walls had rotted through, they had been patched with the tops and bottoms of discarded oil drums. Here and there in the narrow intervals between the buildings, a few stunted bougainvillea bushes struggled valiantly to thrust their way up through the hard-packed earth, and wild corallita vines lent unexpected, incongruous daubs of pastel pink to the grim expanse of rotting wood and metal. Everywhere in the road about the houses there were children, vacant-eyed, listless, pot-bellied, squatting in the dirt or rummaging with the pigs.

Lampit and Cleydon walked together in silence. Presently they turned into a narrow, dirt-paved alley, bordered on either side by a tall patch-work fence of corrugated iron sheets pierced intermittently at eye level with jagged rust holes. The alley was ripe with pig droppings and refuse that had been tossed over the fence from the houses on the other side. Through the rust holes, Cleydon could see a succession of cramped, cluttered, bare-earthed back yards. The sound of fretful children and the tired, angry voices of their mothers drifted over the fence and into the foetid alley.

There was no piped water here. They passed little groups of women and children bearing on their heads kerosene tins full of water which they had fetched from the nearest stand pipe more than a quarter of a mile away. Cleydon noticed that they all seemed to recognise Lampit and they greeted him with undisguised pleasure, their weary, sullen black faces suddenly lit up by a flash of white teeth. In contrast, they looked at Cleydon from beneath their heavy burdens with surprise and unguarded suspicion. They were not used to seeing a white man in that place.

Lampit's house stood at the bottom of the alley. Except for the presence of a few more flowering shrubs and a vast corallita vine which had scaled one side and so concealed the rotting planks that lay beneath it, there was nothing to distinguish this hut and its surroundings from any of those they had passed on the way.

Lampit led the way into the yard through a hole in the picket fence; a gate hung precariously by one broken hinge. On the barren earth behind the house a woman was boiling two breadfruit in a tin which rested on a charcoal fire. Around her, a ring of black children squatted silently in the sun waiting for their midday meal. A hand of green bananas lay on the earth beside the fire, but Cleydon could see no sign of fish or meat. Lampit did not introduce him. He merely nodded in the direction of the woman and said: 'That is my mother; those are my brothers and sisters. Only two of us have the same father, and he doesn't live here now.'

He ushered Cleydon into the little building, determined that he should see it all now that he was here. It did not take long, for there were only two rooms. The family evidently used one of them to eat in, for there was a plain wooden table in the middle with a bench down each side. On the table a condensed milk tin served as a vase and in it someone had dropped a spray of pink corallita taken from the vine outside. Except for an ancient, illustrated calendar suspended from a nail above the doorway, the walls were bare. The calendar was brown with age and the dust of years. The other room was the family bedroom. As Cleydon gazed about that room, it occurred to him that it was scarcely larger than the built-in cupboard of his own room at Illana's Hall in which Thomasina kept his clothes. No doubt, he thought, the same comparison had struck Lampit on that ill-fated visit to New Providence. There were seven rag-filled sacks ranged about the walls. Lampit said in a voice without expression: 'I don't sleep in here with the rest. I sleep in the other room.'

It was the first time he had spoken since they entered the building.

He did not invite Cleydon to sit down or offer him

anything to eat or drink. When the conducted tour of the house was complete, Cleydon said: 'I must get back now to finish my shopping.'

Lampit just nodded and walked with him to the top of the alley. From there Cleydon found his own way back without difficulty. There was no danger that he might lose his bearings: the places they had passed half an hour earlier were stamped indelibly upon his memory and their images were to fade very little over the years ahead. And, curiously, of all his memories of that afternoon, the most deeply etched proved to be the forlorn, incongruous presence of that pale pink spray of flowers in its milk tin vase on the table in Lampit's house.

As he left the noisome slums behind him and approached again the centre of the city with its well dressed white shoppers and its prosperous, complacent ambience, Cleydon felt that he could well have been a traveller returning from another world.

'I want you to know that it is white people like you and all the Langfords before you that cause me and my family to live like this,' Lampit had informed him as they took leave of each other at the top of his alley. 'It is all because you and the rest like you grind us into the dust.'

As he drove home to New Providence across the mountains later that afternoon, Lampit's bitter words echoed and re-echoed in the cavern of Cleydon's mind. He drove slowly and with uncharacteristic care.

'Is it true?' he kept asking himself. 'Are we white Cecilians really to blame for what I saw? Is Lampit right?'

For the first time in his life, Cleydon wished he knew more about where his family had come from and how they had behaved on the journey which had carried them to the affluent position they now held on Saint Cecilia. He cursed the ill luck that had brought him in contact with the black boy once again and which, much against his will, was responsible for the uncomfortable thoughts that now filled his mind.

By the time he braked the Alvis to a halt on the gravel at the front of the marble steps of Illana's Hall, however, his thoughts had already moved on to the more rewarding consideration of which reach of the river he would fish next morning, and – thinking further ahead – of whether it was true, as he had heard, that English girls were a lot more passionate than their cold manner might suggest.

10

Cleydon Langford arrived in England to enter university towards the end of August 1939. It was not an auspicious time. Ten days later he found himself listening on the radio to the weary, disillusioned voice of Neville Chamberlain informing the British people that once again they were at war with Germany.

Cleydon was not an aggressive individual, but it had been brought home to him on the ship which carried him to England that, cocooned on his father's Cecilian estate, his life up to that point had lacked both excitement and challenge. Several of the ship's officers with whom he had made friends were scarcely older than he was, but it was plain to him that without exception they had all seen a great deal more of life. They were too polite to say so, but it was equally plain that as men of the world they thought that Cleydon was still wet behind the ears. The knowledge dismayed him, and the declaration of war seemed to offer an ideal and quite unexpected opportunity to make up lost ground. The war would not last long and he was perfectly prepared – indeed eager – to experience a degree of danger and discomfort. In addition to this, the prospect of the next three years at an English univeristy had grown increasingly unattractive as the commencement of the first term approached. On an impulse, he sought out the nearest recruiting office and joined the British Army.

His active service was brief and undistinguished. On the very day the Wehrmacht invaded Holland and Belgium, he was posted with his regiment to France. His subsequent military experience was confined to the hazards of an army in retreat. As the BEF fell back towards Dunkirk, his company was attacked by forward elements of Rommel's 7th Panzer Division on its way to the sea. At a bleak crossroads in a field of ripening wheat, he was hit by shrapnel in the thigh and taken prisoner. He spent the next five years in various prison camps within the borders of the Third Reich. One of the few letters which safely made the long journey from New Providence to Westphalia during this time was from his father; it told him of his mother's death from cancer in 1943. In March 1945, he was released by the Americans on their way to the Elbe.

He was demobilised in England in the spring of 1946. His only wish was to return to Saint Cecilia at the earliest possible moment. During the aimless, interminable years of his imprisonment he had come to realise for the first time just what the island meant to him and how fortunate he was to have been born there and to have grown up in the splendid setting of New Providence estate. What he had always taken for granted suddenly appeared infinitely precious. The thought now of spending three years at a cold, grey English university had become quite intolerable. In the event, it took nine months for him to secure a passage on a converted troopship bound for the Caribbean, and Cleydon did not arrive home until the week before Christmas.

New Providence was incredibly green with the early rains; between the files of royal palms which flanked the driveway, the poinsettias had erupted in extravagant bursts of scarlet flame. After the drab, monochrome aspect of the English countryside, caught in the toils of an early winter, the riot of colour brought a special joy. The walls of the great white house came into view from the window of the car and his heart swelled with an almost unbearable happiness.

He thought: It's all just as it was when I left; nothing's altered. But he was wrong. He had been away for more than seven years and there were changes everywhere. In the first place, his father was now an old man, frail, querulous and suddenly full of grim predictions about the future of white men on Saint Cecilia. His wife's death three years earlier had desolated him. He was so much older than she had been and the thought that she might die first had never entered his head. He had resigned his honorary position on the Governor's Privy Council and now he rarely left Illana's Hall. He was seventy-eight years old and, so it seemed to Cleydon, nothing in life afforded him pleasure any more.

There were other changes that had taken place during the years of Cleydon's absence that were not at first so easy to discern. The greatest of these was a subtle shift in the attitude of black Cecilians towards the white families of the island, and it was several weeks before he sensed it for himself as he walked on the streets of the capital. The old deference was no longer apparent; black men and women, especially the younger ones, did not trouble to keep to the edge of the pavements any more when white ladies and gentlemen approached. Out of the general unrest of the years immediately before the war, the first black political parties had emerged. Ordinary Cecilians had discovered the power of organised labour. As more than one person had foreseen, the 'martyrs' who in 1938 had fallen on the streets to the rifles of the hard-pressed police gave in death an inspiration to the new movement for equality that no amount of money could have purchased. In 1945, as soon as the war was over, and to the shrill protests of all white Cecilians, the British Government in London had conceded adult suffrage and a certain measure of self-rule. A new Constitution was introduced.

In March the following year general elections to the Assembly in the capital were held for the first time. In a desperate bid to head off the spectre of black men in places of authority, Charles Langford and a group of wealthy friends had formed their own political party and offered themselves as candidates. Charles naturally stood for the constituency in which New Providence lay and, because a large proportion of the registered voters were his own employees, he never doubted for a moment that he would win. His clumsy soundings of public opinion, relayed to him by a handful of sycophantic older labourers, all informed him that he would be chosen. Black men, they assured him, were very well aware that they could never trust people of their own colour to represent them; they really wanted to remain in the paternal care of the Ol' Massa. They knew it was what he wanted to hear, just as well as they knew it was a lie. It is a measure of the distance he had placed between himself and his black labourers that he was sure it was the truth.

In the event, Charles Langford (Conservative Values Party) polled fewer than fifty votes of the four thousand cast, and none of his white colleagues who stood in other parts of the island fared much better. Not a single member of their still-born party was elected to the new Assembly. For the time being, the Constitution still gave the Governor the right to over-rule decisions of the Assembly, but no one was so blind as not to see that this power, too, would soon be conceded. The awful truth could not be disguised: the island at last was firmly on the road to rule by black men. As Charles himself said when he was first brought the news of the result of the election: 'This is the beginning of the end in Saint Cecilia: the niggers have caught the scent of power and they are going to follow their noses like monkeys downwind from a mango tree until they hold the fruit in their hands.' He was not usually so colourful in his speech, but he was right.

He never really recovered from the injury to his self-esteem and to his conviction that it was ordained that white men should forever rule black men in the West Indies. In April 1947 he fell ill. In all his life up to then, he had scarcely known a day's illness and even now his doctors could find nothing specifically wrong with him. He seemed to know instinctively, however, that his life was drawing to its close. The prospect of death had long ceased to hold any terrors for him; indeed, after the humiliation of his foray into politics, he was almost prepared to welcome it. He died in his sleep six months to the day after Cleydon's return from Europe.

He was buried in the family plot which lay within the green walls of an unclipped oleander hedge on the lower slope of the hill behind Illana's Hall. They laid him between his wife and his own father and, at his wish, the simple funeral was attended only by a handful of his closest friends.

It rained on the day Cleydon had chosen and little runnels of ash-grey water raced down the hillside and carried away the untidy edges of the freshly turned soil. The local priest was a melancholy man at the best of times and the sombre words of the funeral service at the graveside were rendered more sombre still by his lugubrious delivery and by the persistent rain, borne down from the mountains by a sharp south-easterly wind.

When it was all over and Cleydon had returned to the house, he did not encourage the mourners to stay, and he dealt briskly with the melancholic priest when the man insisted on remaining behind to offer the comfort of his religion. As soon as he was gone, Cleydon went out to the butler's pantry to give the servants the night off and, by the time darkness had fallen over the fields of New Providence, he found himself alone in the silent house for the first time in his life.

As he left her at the door of the pantry, old Thomasina had said to him: 'Don' grieve too much, Massa Cleydon. Ol' Massa live a long life. He never really wish anyone no harm an' God is merciful . . .'

It was not much of an epitaph, Cleydon reflected later, but it was kindly meant and there was not a great deal more that could be truthfully said about his father. He had done so little with his life. He had been a very wealthy man, and yet he had chosen neither to interest himself in the source of that wealth nor to spend it to any real advantage. Apart from his undemanding duties as a Privy Councillor – and that brief,

ill-considered leap into politics towards the end of his life –
he had been content to remain on his estate surrounded by
those material comforts he could rely on, entertaining with
his wife their closed circle of friends and being entertained by
them.

After his return to Saint Cecilia from England in 1890, he
had never again visited Europe and all his married life he
successfully resisted his wife's periodic attempts to get him to
spend a few weeks in New York, or even at one of those new
resorts which sprang up in quick succession along the east
coast of Florida. He had wanted to stay where he was, and he
had done so.

It seemed to Cleydon, as he thought about it that evening
after the funeral, a pitifully shallow existence for someone
who had held the means to do so much more with his life.

On the morning following the funeral, old Baines the family
solicitor called at New Providence with a copy of Charles
Langford's will. The terms were quite straightforward and
they had been made known to Cleydon immediately after his
return from Europe. Apart from the gift of a few personal
possessions to his father's closest friends – and there were not
many who had outlived him – and the customary bequest of
a month's salary to each of the household servants, the entire
estate passed to Cleydon. There was New Providence itself,
the three much smaller satellite properties, including the one
he loved on the slopes of the Blue Mountains, and a substan-
tial sum of money on deposit in the bank.

The solicitor read through the will and announced that he
would apply for probate in the usual way. He expected no
delay. The meeting was soon over.

'By the way,' the old man said as he stood up to take his
leave, 'I have a letter for you. Your father instructed me to
deliver it after his death.'

He rummaged in his leather briefcase for a moment,
produced a manila envelope addressed in Charles Lang-

ford's large, untidy hand and laid it on the desk.

'Do you know what it's about?' Cleydon inquired.

'Only in general terms,' the solicitor said. 'I think you can regard it as your father's hope for the future of his family.'

He was a frail old man, almost as old as Cleydon's father had been. Cleydon took his arm to help him negotiate the long flight of stairs back to his car at the front of the house.

'Please accept my condolences and those of my firm,' he said formally as his chauffeur held open the door for him. 'Your father and I knew each other for more than fifty years. I hope my firm can continue to serve the family . . .'

Cleydon thanked him; they shook hands and the younger man waited until the car had passed between the ranks of royal palms and was lost among the fields of ripening cane on its way towards the main road and the capital.

He returned to his father's study; *his* study now, as he reminded himself firmly. The letter was still on the desk and his inclination was to leave it there for the time being. He experienced a sudden, unaccountable desire to get out of the house, to take up his rod and line from its place in the hall and to spend the rest of the day alone in his boat on a distant reach of the river that bordered his land. First, however, it was necessary to satisfy his curiosity.

He picked up a heavy mahogany letter opener and slit the flap of the envelope. He saw at once, from the date at the top of the letter, that his father must have written it only a matter of weeks before his own return to Saint Cecilia, and not long after Cleydon had sent to tell him that he was coming home at last.

'My dear Cleydon,' Charles Langford had written in his untidy script, 'There is a matter that has weighed heavily on my mind in recent years. I have committed it to this letter which I have told Baines to pass to you upon my death.

'I shall put it as simply as I can. What I want to say to you is this: for nearly three centuries, our family has kept its racial integrity: we have remained white.

'Now our race has lost its rightful authority in this island, but that is no reason at all why we should not continue to remain separate from the black people our forefathers brought here to serve us from the jungles of Africa.

'If we ever mingle our blood with theirs we shall diminish our worth as human beings. We have a duty to keep faith with all the Langfords who went before us and I rely on you to do so.'

He had signed the letter 'Your affectionate father', and Cleydon recalled how much he had longed for a tangible sign of that affection when he was a child; but with the burden of the letter he could find no quarrel at all.

11

Unlike his father, once Cleydon had inherited his properties he did not intend to allow their management to be exercised by someone else. He pensioned off the attorney and took the reins into his own hands.

It was apparent at once that things were not as they should have been. At New Providence, the factory machinery was worn and largely obsolete; on the satellite estates, the managers had come to realise in recent years that they could do pretty much as they pleased. They had not been visited either by Charles Langford or by the attorney for a very long time and, as a consequence, they had neglected their work. In the banana fields, the walks between the ranks of ripening fruit were choked with weeds which drew off the natural richness of the soil, and this general neglect was quite apparent to Cleydon in the balance sheets of the estates.

He spent the next three years repairing the damage; then he turned his attention to the possibility of raising beef cattle on the empty pasture land at New Providence and decided to try his hand at breeding a more suitable strain of animal than proved to be locally available. Producing the new strain was hard work and, inexorably, it came to take up nearly every minute of his limited spare time. This did not worry him, however, partly because he enjoyed the challenge and partly because it provided him with a very serviceable excuse for not joining the vacuous circuit of cocktail and dinner parties which were so much a feature of his parents' lives. He still went fishing on Sunday mornings and friends called in from time to time in the evenings after dinner. If, just occasionally, he felt lonely living by himself in that beautiful, cavernous house, he was never consciously unhappy.

It was at the beginning of 1949 that Cleydon received a letter from the editor of a popular English magazine saying that he intended to send a journalist to Saint Cecilia later in the year to prepare an article about the island. The editor hoped Cleydon would be willing to allow the man to spend a day at New Providence to see for himself how sugar was produced. He suggested a date.

Cleydon dictated a brief reply to the effect that he had no objection to the proposed visit but that it would be crop time, the mills would be grinding and he doubted very much that he would be able to spare more than ten minutes or so to explain how the factory worked. There had been visiting journalists at New Providence once or twice in the past and his experience with them and their demands on his time had not always been happy ones.

He signed the letter, gave it to his clerk and immediately forgot all about it.

The journalist arrived three months later on a day which had begun badly for Cleydon and was getting progressively worse as the morning wore on. He was closeted with his senior engineer in the engine room of the factory trying to discover the cause of a sudden loss of power to the conveyor belts which carried the cane stalks to the mill. The temperature in that enclosed place was approaching 130 degrees, the clamour of the auxiliary diesel made it impossible for either man to understand what the other was saying, and they both knew that in the factory yard above them hundreds of tons of freshly cut cane were piling up and could be spoiled if the conveyor belts were still idle by the end of the day.

It was into the middle of this scene of misfortune that one of the clerks from the estate office arrived to announce that an English journalist had appeared at the factory and claimed to have an appointment with the owner. Cleydon suddenly recalled the visit to which he had agreed three months earlier.

With murder in his heart he signalled the engineer to carry on for the moment without him, skirted a pool of oil which had leaked from the crank case on to the concrete floor and scrambled out of the engine house. He talked across the open yard towards the office building, his shirt plastered to his back with sweat, his hands blue-black with oil, his temper sorely tried by the knowledge that he could so easily have prevented the unwelcome interruption by saying 'no' to the magazine's original request.

He pushed open the door of his office and found a girl with short blonde hair sitting quietly in the wicker chair beside his desk. For a moment they stared at each other without speaking. Cleydon was suddenly conscious of the fact that his khaki trousers were stained with oil and that there was a broad smear of engine grease running from the lobe of his left ear to the corner of his mouth.

He said the first thing that came into his mind: 'I thought you were going to be a man.'

The girl was not disconcerted. She stood up and held out her hand.

'My name's Pat Stapleton,' she said. 'Our man couldn't come so they sent me instead.'

Without thinking, Cleydon shook her hand.

They spent the next five minutes with a bowl of kerosene and a flannel unsuccessfully trying to remove all trace of oil from her fingers. Flushed with embarrassment, Cleydon fumbled for words of apology; but the girl did not seem to mind at all.

She said in her quiet voice: 'Please don't worry. If I didn't get a bit grubby on an assignment like this, my editor would say I hadn't earned my pay.'

Cleydon relaxed a little and they both laughed. He noticed that her teeth were very white and even and that her smile lifted the corners of her eyes. He decided that the engineer could perfectly well deal with the problem of the conveyor belt without his help and that it would be churlish to have one of the field overseers show the girl around the estate. He thought that he had better do the job himself.

He escorted her through the factory building and they looked down from the catwalk to where the engineer had discovered the cause of the trouble and was about to start the main engine again. Then they watched the giant mills grinding the cane stalks and climbed down the metal ladder to the boiling room where the raw juice simmered wickedly in its copper vats. After that, Cleydon took her out to the fields to see the cutters at work and, in the evening, he drove her back to the hotel in the capital where she had booked a room.

He found himself thinking a lot about her during the course of the next few days, which she spent visiting other parts of the island in obedience to her editor's brief; on the Saturday morning he telephoned her hotel to ask whether she would be interested in having a look at a coffee plantation in the mountains.

At first she said that coffee plantations had not been included in her itinerary; then she said: 'Yes, please, I would like to do that very much,' and Cleydon's heart leapt with a swift, unrestrained surge of pleasure.

He drove her up to the property in the Blue Mountains which he had loved so much as a boy and which, in recent years, he had only too rarely been able to visit. They lit a log fire in the living room and watched the evening mist settle lightly in the branches of the silk cotton trees outside. He had intended to take her back to her hotel before dark, but as the sun went down it began to rain and it seemed only prudent to spend the night where they were.

The rain continued intermittently during the course of the next two days and it was not until Monday evening that they finally drove down from the mountains; by that time it had somehow come to seem ridiculous that she should return to her hotel. She came with Cleydon instead to stay at Illana's Hall. There she wrote the article for which she had been sent to Saint Cecilia in the first place and posted it off to her editor. Attached to it was a note to say that she would not be coming back. Three weeks later, they were married at Illana's Hall beside the waterfall.

Their son, David, was born towards the end of 1950. Cleydon's happiness, however, was muted by the unexpectedly difficult birth. For several weeks afterwards, Pat lay seriously ill in a hospital bed while he watched a succession of grim-faced doctors come and go from her room.

In time, her face lost the waxen pallor which had driven such fear into his heart and she began to recover her strength. The day came at last when he was able to take her home to Illana's Hall, their son cradled in her arms; but it was with the knowledge that they could never attempt to have another child.

In the years that followed, they stayed close to New Providence. Cleydon persuaded old Thomasina to return from her retirement to be David's nurse and, to please him, the woman told anyone who would listen how much the new baby reminded her of his father when he was the same age.

'Massa David have de same sweet temper as his daddy,' she would say, 'an' he even look jus' like him if you view him from de side.'

Cleydon would laugh modestly whenever he heard this flattery; but, as time went by, he did come secretly to believe it and when David was five years old he abandoned his cattle breeding project in order to spend more time with the boy. His reward was to overhear Pat say to a friend that between him and his son there was a very special bond.

Those too-short years of David's childhood were full of happiness for all three of them, clouded for Cleydon only by the realisation that Pat was often in pain and that her doctors could not agree among themselves how best to treat her.

Because, as a family, they found within the boundaries of New Providence all they needed to be content, events taking place beyond their land rarely impinged upon them. Cleydon was aware, of course, that Saint Cecilia was moving inexorably towards independence from colonial rule and, as his father's experience had shown, the days of white authority were numbered. But he could see no reason why any of this should affect the way in which he lived. Both black political parties which had arisen as the war ended were moderate in their views; they advocated no radical social change and they were agreed that the big estates were best left in private hands. They believed their objective of a more just society could be met with time and patience. There were even a few white members on their policy committees. Cleydon was reassured. Black and white, he now felt sure, could continue to live together on the island without any fundamental shift in the nature of their relations with each other. There would be no more need to meet each other socially than there had been in the past. Since that ill-fated day with Lampit at New Providence, Cleydon had never invited a black man to his house, and he had no intention of doing so in the future.

Independence for Saint Cecilia finally arrived at the beginning of 1969. A few months later a black man replaced the British queen as Head of State. To Pat, it all seemed part of a natural, even a desirable process; but the appointment was received with shocked disbelief by the older members of the white community and, although unlike most of them Cleydon had long recognised it as inevitable, on the day of change he, too, found it hard to swallow. He consoled himself with the thought that the changes were essentially cosmetic; beneath the surface things would remain much as they always had been, and on his New Providence estate he had room to distance himself from all those aspects of the

157

new reality which particularly offended him.

It was ironic that the first event to shake his complacency stemmed from an incident which took place not in the West Indies but in the distant Transvaal of South Africa. In May 1969, a crowd of black demonstrators gathered in that country to express their hatred of the pass laws. A party of white policemen opened fire when the demonstrators refused to disperse. As the dust settled, it was seen that more than eighty black men and women lay dead in the roadway. The Pietburg Massacre, as it soon became known, stirred a wave of furious protest throughout the Caribbean. Saint Cecilia was not excepted.

Cleydon first read of the Pietburg incident on the front page of the daily paper. He glanced at the headline, began to read the text that followed, lost interest and turned to the farming pages on the inside. It was the last Saturday of the month, the day he usually drove Pat to the shops in the capital. They planned to have lunch with friends whose house lay in the hills overlooking the city and to return to New Providence before dark.

They set out at about seven o'clock, intending to arrive in the city just before ten. There was not much traffic on the road and they made good time. By half-past nine they were nearing Victoria Square in the centre of the city, on their way to the hotel by the waterfront where Cleydon always left the car. As they approached the square, they could see that a crowd of people had gathered on the central area of grass and was overflowing into the streets immediately around it.

Pat said: 'It looks like they're holding a revival meeting, but I thought they only held those on Sundays . . .' and at that moment Cleydon recalled the headline in the newspaper about the Pietburg incident.

It was too late to turn back and so avoid passing through the middle of the crowd; a long queue of Saturday morning traffic had already built up behind them. The cars ahead were very slowly inching their way through the press of excited people. Cleydon leant back in his seat, lit a rare cigarette and resolved to be patient. Pat, her journalist's curiosity aroused, craned forward to get a better view of what was going on.

At one side of the square a wooden platform had been erected against the plinth of the marble statue of the old Queen which gave the place its name. People had scaled the statue to get a better look at the speakers who had assembled to address them, and one bearded black man with a tri-coloured woollen cap had perched himself with deliberate insolence upon the white marble head. The raucous, electronically distorted voices of the men at the microphone echoed crazily from the walls of the buildings all around them. The meeting, they soon learned, had been called to protest about the South African incident. It was hot, and in the still morning air the earthy reek of many hundreds of sweating black bodies hung heavily over the square.

The queue of cars in which they were trapped crawled painfully forward; as they drew abreast of the platform a new speaker was introduced to the meeting. His name was drowned out by a wave of wild applause which sent the startled pigeons rocketing upwards from their nests in the steeple of the parish church on the other side of the street.

Unlike his predecessors at the microphone, the new speaker did not have to shout to gain the attention of the crowd. His voice was smooth and softly pitched and, when he called for silence so that everyone there could hear what he had to say, an instant hush fell over the restless crowd. People stopped pushing and jostling to secure a better view and stood rooted to the spot on which they found themselves. It was clear that they all knew the identity of the speaker and that they wanted to listen to him. The queue of cars came to a complete standstill, but Cleydon's own view of the platform was obscured by the statue of the old Queen and the people perched around it.

'Brothers and sisters,' the speaker began, 'I am addressing

you as a black man talking to his own. I am not concerned with people of any other colour . . . my words are not for them . . . neither are they for those black politicians who have betrayed us by bringing white men into their counsels . . .'

Instantly Cleydon recognised the voice, deeper now and more resonant than when he had last heard it more than thirty years before, but unmistakable. It was Lampit.

It was soon apparent that he had only recently returned to Saint Cecilia, and he had much to say about his experiences abroad. He spoke first about his early years in England, his humiliation at the hands of white landladies and ticket collectors; of the outrages of the Ku Klux Klan which he had witnessed in Alabama; of the oppression of the African in a part of his own continent; and now of the massacre of black men by white men at Pietburg. In the fury of his resentment, he lapsed unconsciously into the vernacular of the alley in which he was born, the language of the ragged crowd of discontented men and women who had gathered in the square to hear him.

'Now let us look at how t'ings stan' right here in Saint Cecilia,' Cleydon heard him say. 'For t'ree hundred years de white man keep us in chains. Now our time come. We-all can mek dis islan' a black man's paradise, but fus we mus' t'row out de chil'ren of de slave masters . . .'

There was more in the same vein; then slowly, skilfully he began to draw his speech to a close.

'You-all mus' trus' me,' he declared, 'an I will show you how to do it.'

Cleydon heard him take a deep breath.

'Now, brudders an' sisters, jus' remember one more t'ing: wid me you cannot lose.' His tightly controlled voice suddenly leapt a full octave on the scale. 'I am de path to de future,' he yelled.

The claim struck a chord; there was a thunderous roar of approval from the crowd. Pat and Cleydon sat helplessly in their seats, trapped in the middle of several hundred hysterical, aggressive black men and women searching now for an outlet to their fury.

But Lampit had not finished.

'I want you-all to hear one last t'ing,' they heard him yell, his voice echoing across the square with its message of hate. 'De enemy is not only in Sout' Africa; he living right here among us in dis islan'.'

Immediately the car was surrounded by a mob of yelling, gesticulating men and women, their black, sweat-stained faces contorted with rage. Hurriedly Cleydon rolled up the windows and pressed the catches to lock the doors. A bearded man leapt on to the bonnet, produced a length of steel piping from beneath his shirt and deliberately smashed the windscreen in front of Cleydon's face.

'Tun' over de car,' they heard him yell, 'let us tun' over de car.'

At once the chant was taken up by the crowd around him.

An empty beer bottle flew through the air and exploded on the roof immediately above Cleydon's head; shreds of amber glass glinted in the sunlight. Cleydon leant over and pushed Pat roughly out of her seat and beneath the shelter of the instrument panel. There were fragments of shattered windscreen in her hair and upon her bare shoulders; a thin trickle of blood ran down her cheek from a graze on the temple. There was blood, too, on Cleydon's own hands, cut when he threw them up to protect his face from the man with the steel pipe.

At that moment the chant of the crowd was interrupted by a shriller, more urgent cry of 'police comin', and the hostile press of people around the car began to draw back. A party of sweating policemen armed with long wooden batons forced their way through. With difficulty, a passage was opened ahead; the long file of cars began to move forward again. Suddenly they were clear of the crowd and driving down the main street of the city towards the waterfront and the hotel.

A few white shoppers on the pavements, unaware of the meeting in the square two hundred yards away, looked up curiously at the Bentley's shattered windscreen, and the breeze from the harbour blowing up the street was unnaturally cool against their faces; otherwise, for Pat and Cleydon it might once again have been any other Saturday shopping expedition and the brief, ugly incident in the square merely an unpleasant daydream.

They did not stop in the city that morning, however. Cleydon turned off the main street, left along the waterfront, and drove out between the shops and the houses into the foothills behind them, towards the place where they were expected for lunch later that day. The narrow, winding country road was deserted. At a sharp bend where it overlooked the capital, Cleydon pulled in to the shade of a julie mango tree and switched off the engine of the car. In the silence that followed, he could hear the soft, familiar call of a mountain dove and the swift rush of the stream which traversed the road behind them to plunge steeply into the valley below. The sickly-sweet stench of fallen mangoes was heavy on the air. Pat threw herself into his arms.

'Did you see their faces, darling?' she asked. 'They hate us. Those people really hate us.'

Cleydon climbed out of the car, walked back to the stream and dipped his handkerchief into the cool, crystal water. Very gently, he wiped away the thin line of crusted blood at her temple and brushed the glass from her hair.

'I don't think many of the ordinary people hate us,' he said at last. 'They just didn't know what they were doing; blacks are like that. It is the speaker who was to blame.'

'Well, he certainly hates us,' she said sadly. 'I wonder who he is and why he feels that way.'

'I know who he is,' Cleydon replied, 'and I'm afraid that he has his reasons.'

In the days that followed, he took the trouble to discover just what Lampit had done with his life since that well-remembered day back in 1939 which was the last occasion on which their paths had crossed.

Lampit had spent the war years as an undergraduate at Oxford. He had done very well there. Once again that formidable combination of natural ability and the cold determination to succeed had led him forward.

In 1948 he had left for Africa, and quite soon afterwards his name was being mentioned with those of Kenyatta and Nkrumah and the other black men whose fight for the independence of their countries was just beginning. Lampit's education in the law, and his quick intelligence, were invaluable to them and his name soon found its way on to the Colonial Office's list of Undesirable Immigrants who were banned from visiting the African colonies because they stirred up trouble. He settled down in London and, when they needed his advice, the black leaders sought it there.

His reputation and influence grew steadily during the course of the next ten years. In 1957, he was a prominent guest at the independence celebrations of Ghana, the first of the African colonies to win its freedom. It was the high honour paid him there that demonstrated just how important was the role he had played behind the scenes. At one of the public functions held during the week of celebrations, the new Prime Minister insisted that Lampit should be seated at his side; a picture of the two of them, their hands raised together in triumph at the end of white rule, appeared on the pages of newspapers in many parts of the world.

In the wild euphoria of the occasion, Lampit permitted himself to be interviewed by an American Negro magazine. He made no attempt to conceal his intense satisfaction that the European domination of the African continent was drawing to a close; then he was asked what the future held for his own country, Saint Cecilia.

He needed no time to consider his answer; it was the subject which above all others, he said, had dominated his

163

thinking and guided his actions since he was old enough to recognise the white man's oppression of the black.

'I intend to transform the island,' he announced. 'When the time comes, I shall make it a black man's paradise.'

It was the very phrase he had used to Cleydon in their classroom at that school in the mountains of Saint Cecilia, more than twenty years earlier. And it was clear to Cleydon that the intervening years had only served to strengthen his belief in that chilling, messianic vision.

Lampit's private life had been more mundane and less successful. He had married once but, to his intense disappointment, his Jamaican wife had produced no children; to make up for this he had brought up one of his nieces as his own daughter. It was said that she was the only human being he loved more than himself. He had divorced his wife while he was in Africa; he had not married again.

He had returned to Saint Cecilia on the day of its independence with the carefully timed announcement that his work in Africa was now complete and that he had come home to stay. He vigorously protested at what he found there. Although the government of the island was now effectively in the hands of black men, they were not at all the kind of men he approved of. Real power, he said, economic power, still rested in the hands of the white landowners. The island's loudly proclaimed independence was a sham; real independence would only be achieved when the land, which had been watered over the centuries by the blood of black people, was owned at last by the descendants of those same people who had made it bloom. In the new Saint Cecilia, he said, there could be no room for more than one race; the children of the slave masters must be ejected.

The public meeting to protest against the Pietburg Massacre, the same meeting in which Pat and Cleydon had been unwillingly caught up, had given him his first opportunity to make known his views in person to every black Cecilian. Following that meeting and the next morning's newspaper reports of what was said, Lampit's opinions and ambitions were soon the topic of all serious discussion in every house and rum bar all over the island.

It had been widely predicted on his return to Saint Cecilia that Lampit would create his own political party which he would employ, in due course, to secure for himself the position of power that had always been his secret aim. The prediction proved false; he chose instead to build a trade union. It was a characteristically shrewd decision: the two existing political parties were, for the time being at least, well entrenched; but such unions as existed were, in contrast, weak and constantly at war with one another. A strong union, open to every worker no matter what his job, would soon generate for him the broadly based support that would be necessary when the time came to make his bid for political power. That, so he told his intimates, was how it had been done in other places; and, through his services in Africa, he had brought with him to Saint Cecilia a considerable sum of money – sufficient, in fact, to allow him to promise to his members such golden things as strike pay and sickness benefits which most black Cecilians had never imagined possible before.

The new union proved to be an instant success; many thousands of workers all over the island abandoned their old, ineffectual organisations and came over to Lampit, lured not so much by his turbulent personality as by the concrete promises he made them of better times ahead.

Not long after the launch of his union, he held another meeting in Victoria Square, the place where Pat and Cleydon had heard him speak less than a year before. The press of people who gathered to applaud him this time was so great that they filled every street leading off the square. He had called the meeting, he announced, to make known the first of his priorities: it was to improve the inhuman lot of the labourers on the island's great estates.

The daily paper next morning faithfully reported his

words. His aim was at least blessed with the virtue of simplicity: everyone could clearly understand it. He intended, as he put it, to squeeze the parasitic white landowners until they vomited the land which belonged to black Cecilians; then it would be distributed to every family which wanted land of its own and could afford none.

As far as the white families were concerned, his intentions were just as plain. 'We are going to make their lives a kind of hell on this island,' he promised. 'We want them to leave and we will not rest until they do. With all my heart I long for the day when I can move from one end of the island to the other and never see a single white face. Only when that time arrives will black men have regained what is owed to them.'

Next day it became obvious to Cleydon that his own property was not only numbered among those selected to bear the brunt of Lampit's first offensive, but that for some reason New Providence had been singled out for special attention. Lampit forced a poll of all employees on Cleydon's estates; his new union won with ease. No sooner had the result been declared than Cleydon was presented with a demand to double the wage of every man and woman on his payroll by the end of the year; and that, it was made clear, was merely a faint taste of what he could expect in the months ahead. There would be no holds barred, there could be no talk of compromise; relief could be purchased only by surrender. The white men must go.

All this, however, was abruptly driven from Cleydon's mind by Pat's sudden illness.

12

Cleydon had known all the time that Pat had never really made a full recovery from the effects of David's birth but, with the passage of the years, her doctors had grown increasingly hopeful that the trouble had been stemmed.

By Christmas 1970, however, she was once again critically ill and for eight days he sat by the side of her hospital bed watching in hopeless agony as she slipped away from him. Cleydon and David were left to face the prospect of the rest of their lives without her joyful presence.

The first twelve weeks were the hardest to bear. After that, they began to find comfort in the recollection of the happy years and of special moments etched in their memories. The bond between father and son, tested now in the fire of a terrible grief, grew stronger than ever, and in David's fair hair and the way his smile lifted the corners of his eyes, Cleydon could find something of what he had lost.

At Pat's insistence, David had been allowed to grow up at New Providence without any of the parental restrictions that had prevented his father from playing with the children of the black estate employees when he was a boy. It was not something that Cleydon liked, but Pat, who could never share his own conviction that black people were somehow less than white ones, felt that David should be free to decide for himself who would be his friends.

From the beginning, Cleydon was uneasy about the fact that his son attached no more significance to the colour of another boy's skin than to the shape of his ears. There were white children, too, on the estate at that time, the sons and daughters of the senior engineer, but David seemed to feel no special kinship with them. His closest companion during the years of his childhood was the ragged son of old Ezekial, the black cowman who had charge of the estate's prize bull.

Watching David one afternoon as he played with his friends along the bank of the stream beyond the lawn, old Thomasina said happily to Cleydon: 'Massa, dat pretty chile is colour blind; him can't see no difference between black and white.'

Because he loved Thomasina, Cleydon smiled; but he was not pleased.

'He will learn in good time,' he said. 'He is still young.'

'Yes, Massa,' Thomasina replied dutifully, but for the rest of the day that brief conversation with his old nurse stayed rooted uncomfortably in Cleydon's mind.

Pat and Cleydon had arranged for David to be tutored privately at New Providence until he was eleven years old. There were no suitable day schools within a reasonable distance of the estate and they would not send him away while he was still scarcely more than a baby. After his eleventh birthday, however, and not without misgivings on Cleydon's part, they took him off to the school in the mountains which Cleydon had attended himself.

Outwardly, the school was much as Cleydon remembered it; but just as Lampit had predicted all those years ago, it was now predominantly black. In the annual photograph still taken, Cleydon noted, with the grim facade of the assembly hall forming the backdrop, it was the few white faces which now seemed oddly out of place in the sea of black ones. Cleydon was suddenly fearful that his son might suffer because of his colour, just as Lampit had suffered on account of his.

As it turned out, he need not have worried. Exactly as he had done at New Providence, David chose his friends without the smallest regard for the colour of their skins; they, in turn, appeared to find nothing remarkable in the fact that he was white. In spite of this – or perhaps because of it – Cleydon was disquieted in a way he could not fully explain even to himself. Pat, for her part, was entirely happy that the hateful virus of racial prejudice had been rejected by her son.

When David came home to New Providence for a weekend in the middle of his first term at school, Cleydon decided to raise the subject with him, choosing his words, as he thought, with much care. Was he really comfortable, he inquired, having to eat and sleep next to boys whose skin was as black as old Thomasina's?

In later years, Cleydon never forgot the way that David looked at him, as though he had not understood the question.

'But why not, dad?' the boy had replied. 'Why shouldn't I be? This is Saint Cecilia, not South Africa. It doesn't matter what colour you are here.' And there was that expression in his blue eyes, half exasperated, half amused, which always reminded Cleydon of Pat. 'I don't care if a boy's puce with yellow stripes as long as he can hold a cricket bat.'

Cleydon forced himself to laugh with his son; but he did not feel amused. The fault, he knew, had been his own. He should never have agreed with Pat to allow David to mix freely with the black children of the estate when he was too young to understand. He had nothing against black people, Cleydon reminded himself, but, as his father used to say, they were somehow 'less than us'. It was a matter one spoke about more discreetly than of old, but it remained as true as it had ever been. The Langfords were a white West Indian family, they had remained white for nearly three hundred years, and Cleydon was determined that they should remain so for ever.

David left school when he was eighteen. He had done far better there than his father thirty years earlier, both in the classroom and on the playing field. His headmaster was generous in his praise of the boy: 'Your son is the kind of man this island is going to need,' he told Cleydon. 'You have every reason to be proud of him.'

Because the headmaster was a coloured man himself, Cleydon received the words without comment: a coloured man, to his mind, had no business passing judgement on a white one; nevertheless, and in spite of his distaste, he felt his heart swell a little with pride and affection. And he had not attempted to dissuade Pat from seeking out each member of staff and thanking them all in her charming, open way for the care and interest they had taken over the matter of her son's education.

To the headmaster, she said: 'You have confirmed David in his childhood conviction that we all belong to one family. Thank you especially for doing that . . .'

A few weeks after the end of that last term, Cleydon had raised with his son the matter of his going on to university. They had discussed the matter generally in the past and Cleydon had taken it for granted that David had in mind an English university. On this point, however, he was mistaken: David wanted to go to the University of the West Indies in Jamaica, where there were already a number of undergraduates from Saint Cecilia.

It was Pat who eventually persuaded Cleydon to let David have his own way in the matter. 'I believe it's really something we have to allow him to decide for himself,' she said quietly. 'He's eighteen years old and he wouldn't have made a choice like that without thinking it all through very carefully.'

Reluctantly, Cleydon agreed and David had left for Jamaica at the beginning of the next university term. He was in his final year there when Pat died on the first day of 1971.

It was not long afterwards that Lampit began in earnest his promised campaign to dislodge the white landowners of Saint Cecilia. Cleydon was able to take some comfort in the knowledge that at least David, several hundred miles away in Jamaica, was not exposed to the bitterness and hostility that he soon experienced. At first he nurtured the hope that by the time his son returned to Saint Ceciila after sitting his final examinations, the trouble might have run its course. As the weeks passed, however, this hope began to seem more and more forlorn.

At New Providence the trouble took the form of a repeated cycle of intimidation followed by strikes and then by senseless, indiscriminate acts of violence. Cleydon refused to give an inch; but when the trouble was extended to the neighbouring estate of his father's friend, Marcus Granville, the frightened old man promptly capitulated. He put his land up for sale and left at once for the prospect of a more peaceful end to his days in the Transvaal of South Africa. The niggers there, he announced, still had a proper respect for white men. Not surprisingly Lampit was quick to hail the departure as a splendid victory – the beginning of the great white exodus to come.

Old Granville's spineless surrender merely bolstered Cleydon's refusal to be intimidated. No black man, he was determined, would ever succeed in forcing him off his land; and so, when his resolve became apparent to Lampit, New Providence was subjected to a new wave of violence. His prize Red Poll bull was discovered dead in its stall one morning, a pitchfork driven through its belly. Ten days later, fire broke out in the sugar factory just before daybreak; they were able to save the engine room and most of the building, but many tons of stored sugar were lost before the blood-red flames were finally brought under control. A thick pall of choking, acrid smoke hung over Illana's Hall that day and, when at last it was dispersed by the rising wind, Cleydon saw that the smoke had left an ugly tracery of blue-black stains upon the white walls of his house.

There was a brief lull after that; then in the second week of August 1971, very early on the day they should have started the mills grinding to crush the first cane of the new season, New Providence was invaded by an army of young toughs despatched from Lampit's headquarters in the capital. The surprise was complete: they arrived unheralded, swarmed into the factory and ejected without ceremony the few labourers who had been brave enough to turn up for work.

Two of the men scaled the roof of the factory and draped a banner over the north wall. From where he stood on the verandah of Illana's Hall, his body trembling with a terrible fury, Cleydon could clearly make out the coal-black lettering: AWAY WITH THE SONS OF THE SLAVE MASTERS, it read.

Immediately his thoughts were of his father and of the old man's fears for the future of white men on Saint Cecilia once the strings of authority had slipped from their fingers. It was just this kind of outrage he had sensed would take place, and Cleydon recalled that he himself had been naive enough to predict that such things could never come to pass. If for no other reason than that he had once known Lampit well, he should have shown more foresight.

He strode into his study and picked up the telephone to call the local police; then it dawned upon him that summoning the police was not going to solve the problem; in a sense, it was an admission of defeat. Immediately he knew what had to be done.

A nervous little group of servants had gathered at the foot of the balustraded steps as he left the house; he saw that old Thomasina's face was wet with tears. He climbed into the Bentley and drove down one of the overgrown, disused tracks which ran between two fields of cane until it met the main road to the capital. The men on the roof of the factory, posted there to gauge his reaction to what was happening, did not see him go.

He swung the car on to the main road; as he approached the entrance gates to New Providence about half a mile further on, a party of bearded men with the bright metal badges of Lampit's union on their shirts recognised the car. Cleydon had taken them by surprise because they had thought that he was still besieged at Illana's Hall. The men gave a collective yell of fury and reached for a stock of missiles which they had cached at the edge of the road. Cleydon put his foot hard down on the accelerator; as he swept past a volley of empty beer bottles ricochetted off the broad lid of the boot. The curses of the men were muted by the rising note of the engine.

It normally took a little over two hours to drive to the capital; on this occasion Cleydon managed it in an hour and thirty-three minutes. And all during that time, the same question kept revolving in his mind, insistently demanding an answer which he could not give: why had Lampit chosen to single him out above everyone else as the particular object of his loathing?

Cleydon arrived in the capital of the middle of the morning. The square in which, with Pat, he had received the first taste of what was to follow at Lampit's hands was almost deserted now; two small boys wrestling on the parched grass and an old man selling water coconuts from a decrepit donkey cart seemed to have it all to themselves. Above the pigeon-fouled head of the Queen-Empress, the air quivered with heat.

Cleydon drove directly to Lampit's office on the waterfront. He took the lift up to the suite on the top floor of the building. The lift was air conditioned and the pile of its fawn carpet was thick beneath his feet. Outside the door of Lampit's office a large black bodyguard lounged in a chair; Cleydon brushed past him and walked in.

Lampit's secretary was a black girl with her hair cut close to the scalp in the current African fashion; she recognised him at once.

He said: 'I have come to see Mr Lampit.' The girl made a play of studying a list of names on her desk.

'You don't have an appointment,' she said at last. 'Mr

Lampit will not see anyone without an appointment.'

Cleydon gripped the edge of her desk with both hands and leant towards her. 'Either you tell him I am here,' he said grimly, 'or I will open that door behind your chair and do it for you.'

The girl's bravado failed her; without another word she stood up, opened the mahogany panelled door in the wall and disappeared. Outside in the corridor Cleydon could hear the bodyguard pacing the floor. He began to pace the floor himself.

The girl returned and said sulkily without looking at him: 'Mr Lampit will give you five minutes of his time.'

She fed a sheet of headed paper into her typewriter and began to hammer at the keys. Cleydon waited in silence to be summoned.

Ten minutes later the door behind the desk opened again. A tall black man dressed in a pale grey suit stood framed in the doorway. The thin, ascetic face had fleshed out, there were two large gold rings on the fingers of his left hand and an aroma of sandalwood and Havana cigars hung about him, but there was no doubt that it was Lampit.

He did not offer to shake hands; in fact in his secretary's presence he gave no sign that he and Cleydon had ever met before. With an imperious wave he beckoned Cleydon into his office. The gold rings gleamed softly in the subdued light. Over his shoulder he said curtly to his secretary: 'Tell my driver to have the car waiting at the front. I will not be long.' Then he closed the door behind them.

Cleydon looked about him. A heavy mahogany desk stood on a raised platform in the most distant corner of the large room; it was apparent that a visitor would be obliged to advance across a vast expanse of pale cream carpet under Lampit's critical gaze before he could hope to speak to him. For some reason Cleydon had been spared that particular ordeal.

The walls of the room were panelled in red cedar and upon

them, in ornate gilt frames, hung signed photographs of more than a dozen African leaders. The photographs were inscribed to Lampit with extravagant expressions of respect and admiration. One notorious President-for-Life had written across the bottom of his portrait: 'To my dear brother and comrade in the struggle against the common enemy . . .'

Cleydon had no doubt who the common enemy might be.

Gathered on a long ebony table beneath the cluster of photographs there was a bizarre collection of African artifacts. Some were beautiful and unmistakably valuable; others poorly worked, tawdry and vulgar. They were displayed together on the polished table without discrimination. Beside a fine bronze head from Benin, Cleydon noticed a cheap glass ashtray decorated with a hand-coloured view of the market place in Kampala.

On the floor of the room, as though guarding access across the thick pile of the carpet to the raised desk, there were half a dozen leopard skins, each head preserved by the native taxidermist's uncertain art with teeth bared in the snarl of defiance with which the unfortunate animal must have met its death.

In its curious, tasteless way it was all very impressive; but what really caught and held the eye – and so no doubt fulfilled its purpose – was the oil painting which hung behind Lampit's desk. It reached clear from the ceiling to the floor and it dominated that room. As Cleydon followed in Lampit's wake across the carpet, he knew immediately that he had seen something very like it once before. Then, with a swift shock of recognition, he realised that he was looking at a giant reproduction of that colourful illustration of Chaka, the Zulu king, which had decorated the cover of one of those books that Lampit used to read so avidly in his spare time at school. The memory of that distant afternoon when he had picked that particular book out of the dust of the school yard and returned it to the injured Lampit was still as fresh and vivid as if it had happened yesterday; it was one memory of his schooldays that time had never dulled. He recalled how the blood had dripped from the black boy's injured lip and how the raucous shouts of the white bully who had tripped him on the stairs echoed across from the cricket field.

On the day he returned to Saint Cecilia, Lampit had ordered the picture copied in oils, and to celebrate the launch of the trade union that was to carry him to power, he hung it on the wall behind his desk. Cleydon found it difficult to resist the thought that, in some strange fashion, Lampit believed that the mantle of Chaka, that champion of the Negro race, had already fallen about his own shoulders. Looking at the picture, it seemed to Cleydon that the artist, by accident or design, had incorporated some of Lampit's own features in the proud and arrogant face of the black king.

Lampit motioned his visitor to a seat at the giant desk and took his own place in the black leather armchair beneath the painting. In his soft voice, stripped now of all trace of the alley where he was born, he said: 'Let us not waste time on pleasantries we do not mean. What is it you want of me?'

'Why have you sent your people to invade my land?' Cleydon demanded.

Lampit made no attempt to answer the question. Instead, he said: 'I am going to give you some advice, Langford, and I shall offer it only once. Leave Saint Cecilia and go where your own people live.'

With a great effort, Cleydon kept a grip on his temper.

'My people, as you call them, have lived on this island for four hundred years,' he replied. 'My own family have been here for more than half that time. It is our home; why should we leave now?'

Lampit leant back in his leather chair and looked over Cleydon's head at the portraits of his admirers on the wall.

'I have never minced words,' he said. 'The truth is that we do not want people of your colour here any longer. There is no place for you in a black man's paradise.'

'Why not?' Cleydon demanded.

'Because you remind us of our past,' Lampit said simply.

At once Cleydon started to protest; Lampit held up his hand.

'If you will take my advice, I will see that no harm comes to you or your property before you leave,' he said. 'I have no wish to see you hurt; I only want you to go.'

His gaze shifted from the pictures on the wall to Cleydon's face.

'If you are stubborn,' he added quietly, 'you will live to regret it.'

It was that unvarnished threat which served to release the pent-up flood of Cleydon's fury. No black man had ever threatened him before. It was a long time since he had last raised his voice in anger and there was much he wished to say. He half expected Lampit to summon the bodyguard from the passage outside. Cleydon's outburst, however, left the black man quite unmoved behind the fastness of his desk. He waited patiently until Cleydon had finished.

'I can see that you do not understand,' he said at last. 'Well, I will try to help your understanding. Listen carefully: for three hundred years my people were held by your people as slaves; we were chattels, bought and sold in the market place like cattle. Now we have to live with that knowledge and those of us who have discovered pride in our blackness, in the fact that we survived the worst that you could do to us, we find the sight of a white man hard to bear. You see, you hurt us too much.'

'Do you believe that black people were the only ones to suffer in these islands?' Cleydon asked. 'Do you think that my ancestors did not have to struggle to survive?'

'There is a difference,' Lampit replied. 'You were never chattels. Some of you may have been convicts or servants, but you were never chattels to be bought and sold like animals at the whim of another human being. Perhaps it is a difference only a black man can understand.'

177

Cleydon had never thought of it like that before. Perhaps Lampit was right, he conceded: there *was* a difference. He returned to the matter that had caused him to seek out the man.

'I want to know why you have singled out New Providence for your attentions. What have I ever done to you?'

For a long moment there was silence in that room. Behind the cedar panelling the air conditioner made a soft, liquid murmur. It was a very comfortable office. Lampit gripped the broad arms of his chair.

'There is something I never told you when we were at school together,' he said at last. 'I am going to tell you now.'

His eyes were curiously unfocussed and his voice was suddenly pitched so low that Cleydon had to crane forward in his seat to catch the words.

'My grandmother was born a slave,' Lampit said. 'She carried her owner's brand upon her breast. When I was a small boy she showed me the mark. She was a very old woman then, but the scar was still painful. I asked her what it felt like when the iron touched her skin. She told me.'

He paused, and Cleydon could see that, in spite of the even tone of his voice, the veins were standing out like cords against the black skin of his neck. It was clear that the man was controlling himself only with the greatest effort.

'She was only eight years old when they branded her,' he continued, 'scarcely more than a baby. She never forgot the touch of the brand for a single day, and neither have I. The hurt was too great.'

'Why are you telling me this?' Cleydon demanded. 'I am sorry about the branding, but all that is history. What has it got to do with me?'

Lampit took a deep breath.

'I will tell you,' he said. 'The scar was in the form of the letter L. The L stood for Langford. My grandmother was your family's chattel; you branded her.'

He released his breath in a long, whistling sigh. 'It is like I said; you remind us of our past.'

In the silence of that followed, try as he might Cleydon could think of nothing further to say. Lampit looked at his watch. The meeting was clearly at an end. He got up, retraced his steps across the broad expanse of carpet, between the snarling leopard heads, and let himself out of the office. His secretary did not trouble to look up when Cleydon followed half a minute later.

Cleydon drove back towards the uncertain sanctuary of Illana's Hall. He was suddenly very tired. The main road to New Providence followed faithfully the original Arawak trail which his great-grandfather William had taken as a boy on that day in 1779 when the family first arrived in Saint Cecilia as refugees from Grenada. It was the same William, as he knew now, who years later had caused the branding of Lampit's grandmother and hundreds like her. At least, he thought wearily, now I can understand what drives the man.

The road ran down from the foothills of the mountain range towards the familiar coastal plain and, not long afterwards, the tall limestone gateposts of the estate entrance came in to view. The bearded group of union trouble-makers was still there, so he returned to Illana's Hall the way he had left, up the narrow dirt road and through the fields of cane.

Thomasina was waiting for him at the top of the marble steps. He thought she was going to give him news of the occupation of the factory, but he was wrong.

'Massa,' she said without preamble. 'Massa David telephone from university. He ask you to call him when you come in. It soun' like him have some good news to tell you.'

'What kind of good news is it?' Cleydon asked. 'God knows, we need some.'

The old woman smiled her gap-toothed smile.

'Is best he tell you himself,' she said. 'It have somethin' to do wid a young lady . . .'

Cleydon said wearily: 'You should have told him to study his books, not the young ladies . . .'

Thomasina giggled. 'Massa, you forgettin'. I always say de chile tek after his daddy.'

Cleydon was suddenly anxious. 'Did you tell him anything about the trouble we are having here?' he asked.

Thomasina shook her head. 'I didn' want him to know, Massa. He would only worry 'bout you. Sufficient time for all dat after he come back.'

Cleydon nodded approvingly. 'You did right. None of this is his quarrel.'

He had not spoken to David in Jamaica for more than three weeks, knowing that he was in the middle of his final examinations. He went up now to his study, told Thomasina to bring him a pink gin and looked at the calendar on his desk. Circled in red on that day's date was a note he had made many months ago: *David's last exam today.*

He dialled the international operator and put through a call to the university in Kingston. As usual, the line was not good; when he was finally connected, David sounded a very long way away.

'How did the exams go?' he asked. 'My calendar says you sat the last one today.'

'The finals were all right, I think,' he heard his son say above the crackle and spit of the interference on the line. 'The last one was this afternoon; the consensus is it might have been worse . . .' Cleydon heard him draw a deep breath. 'But that wasn't the reason I called you . . .' he continued. 'I'm coming home on Saturday . . . I wanted to tell you . . .' – there was a long pause – 'I've met someone . . . I want to marry her . . . I decided to keep the news until the exams were over in case you thought . . . I'm so happy, dad . . .'

His voice was lost in a swift burst of static. Cleydon's view of the green lawns beyond the window and the silver thread of the stream which lay across them was suddenly misted over. Ever since Pat's death he had suffered horribly from the irrational fear that, after leaving university, David might be tempted to drift away on his own for a year or two. The prospect of being left without him at Illana's Hall had filled him with dread. Marriage, he thought now, would settle him down and bind him to New Providence; he could grow old surrounded by his son's family. There would be none of the loneliness which had made his own father's last years so desolate. His heart leapt with an unrestrained surge of joy.

The line cleared.

'Who is it, David?' he managed to ask through the constriction around his throat. 'Do I know her family?'

The reply was masked by a return of static on the line. 'I can't hear you,' Cleydon shouted into the mouthpiece of his telephone. 'Speak up.'

David raised his voice, and at that moment the interference faded once again.

'Her name's Diana,' Cleydon heard him say with perfect clarity. 'Diana Lampit. Her uncle's the trade unionist. Her parents are dead and he's her guardian. He's back in Saint Cecilia now. She's been in my year at the university . . .'

It was suddenly very dark and very cold in Cleydon's study. He sat down heavily in the arm chair, a band of steel tightening around his chest, forcing the air from his lungs. A giant, implacable hand grasped his stomach, turning it in upon itself, squeezing, wrenching, tearing at the muscles of his diaphragm until he groaned in agony.

'Dad,' he heard David's voice say from the receiver in his hand, 'I want you to meet her when we fly home on Saturday . . . she could stay the weekend with us . . .' Then, when there was no reply, Cleydon heard him say to someone evidently standing at his side: 'I think we've been cut off, but no matter. He'll expect us on Saturday . . . now perhaps we better 'phone your uncle . . .'

Very slowly and deliberately Cleydon replaced the receiver on its cradle; he was suddenly desperate for the lost comfort of Pat's arms.

Cleydon could not sleep at all that night; and when he rose as usual at first light next morning, red-eyed and exhausted, he found that the siege of his estate had been called off and the crippling strike was at an end. From the window of his bedroom he could see the labourers streaming back to their jobs, no longer in fear of intimidation by the union men.

By eight o'clock, the factory furnaces had been re-lit and the estate fell back at once into the old, familiar routine of making sugar. There was no sign at all of the offensive banner that had flown from the roof of the factory. Cleydon suddenly recalled how, on the telephone the previous evening, he had overheard David and his black girl planning to tell Lampit about their love for each other; it occurred to Cleydon for the first time that the news must have been quite as shattering for Lampit as it had been for him. No doubt the shame of having the niece he loved engaged to marry a white man and, worse, the son of a man he detested, had prompted Lampit to call off his harassment of New Providence. Nothing else could have done it.

David returned to Saint Cecilia on Saturday morning with Lampit's niece. He collected his old MG from the garage in the capital where he had left it and, with the girl, drove straight to New Providence. They arrived in the middle of the day.

From the window of his study Cleydon watched as the car approached between the ranks of royal palms that flanked the long driveway; although he could not yet see it, the presence of the little vehicle was betrayed by a thin plume of limestone dust thrown into the air as the car disturbed the bone dry surface of the road. In the past, he had always hurried down to the foot of the steps to greet his son when he returned at the end of each university term, but this time he could not bring himself to do it. Instead, he waited alone in the shadow of the entrance to the marble hall.

The car drew up at the front of the house. He watched as David sprang out with that loose-limbed grace he had inherited from his mother. The boy opened the door for his companion.

The girl was dressed in a simple white cotton frock. She wore white sandals and there was a bright purple scarf caught by a silver ring at her neck. The small blaze of colour seemed to emphasise the deep copper pigment of her skin. She was tall and slim, her hair cut short in an oval which framed her face. David took her hand and led her up the steps to meet his father.

He said: 'Dad, this is Diana. For some curious reason she has just agreed to marry me.'

Cleydon looked intently at the girl; instantly he experienced a most vivid recollection of her uncle standing in that very place at the top of the steps more than thirty years earlier, gauche and unsmiling as Cleydon attempted to introduce him to his parents.

Lampits niece was quite different. She was softly spoken, but she carried herself with a quiet air of self-assurance. Cleydon noticed how white her teeth were against the dark velvet of her skin.

'How do you do, Mr Langford,' she said. 'Thank you for letting David bring me here to meet you. He has told me so much about Illana's Hall.'

Cleydon fumbled for the conventional words of greeting, but they seemed to stick in his throat. The girl did not appear to notice. She was relaxed and unselfconscious. Impulsively, she reached over to David and took his hand.

'Now that we are going to get married,' she said, 'I want to learn to love the people David loves.'

It would not have been difficult that weekend for Cleydon to have succumbed to the girl's quiet charm, but he had decided from the beginning that he would make no secret of his disapproval. Any other course, he told himself, would mark him down as a hypocrite. One way or another he intended to restore to his son a proper sense of values and so bring the engagement to an end. It was his duty as a father.

Not long after dinner that night the girl tactfully excused herself, kissed David goodnight and went upstairs to bed. Cleydon fetched a decanter of brandy and two glasses and sat with his son on the verandah of their house. An uneasy silence settled over the two men; in the darkness beyond the stream an owl called; a pair of horseshoe bats passed across the face of the quarter moon.

David was the first to speak.

'I am sorry that my engagement has failed to please you,' he said quietly. 'It would have been easier to have kept it from you for a while, but I didn't want to do that.'

'I am glad you didn't,' Cleydon replied. 'We have never believed in keeping things from each other, you and I.'

David nodded his agreement. In the pale half light that issued from the entrance to the hall, Cleydon was suddenly reminded of how much his son looked like Pat.

'You know that I have nothing against black people,' he continued, 'but I am not going to pretend that I would choose one of them for a daughter-in-law. You are my son, and I am going to tell you how I feel. The fact is that we Langfords are a white West Indian family. After three hundred years in the Caribbean we have every reason to be proud of it. In its own way, this house we live in is evidence of our determination to remain pure: if old Jonas had compromised on this same matter, you and I would be coloured men. I don't believe in the mingling of the races, and neither did any of the Langfords who came before us. We have been obliged to give the Negroes political power in Saint Cecilia, but God knows we don't have to marry them.'

David listened without interrupting. From within the marble hall the soft whisper of the waterfall drifted out into the night. Above their heads, the lamp of a single errant fire-fly went on and off like an aerial lighthouse in the darkness. The distant owl called his mate for a second time. Cleydon felt compelled to say more, to give reasons for his views.

'She is a nice girl,' he went on, ' a beautiful girl in her own way. I can understand why you find her attractive. Sleep with all her by all means if you want to, but don't marry her, David. I don't want coloured descendants any more than old Jonas did. I don't want my grandchildren to have thick lips and flat noses. By all means take her to bed, but for God's sake don't marry her.'

It was an impassioned plea; another long silence settled over them. On the lower slopes of the mountains to the east, Cleydon could make out little wavering pinpoints of yellow light where the charcoal burners and their dogs had camped for the night in the forest. The sweet, blended fragrance of jasmine and pink oleander was heavy on the still air. In the wicker chair opposite, David sat very upright; Cleydon mistook his continued silence for reluctant agreement. David, he thought, was always receptive to reasoned argument; it was not going to be so difficult after all.

Then David spoke, and there was in his voice a quality which Cleydon had never heard before.

'You may be my father,' he said, 'but you are also a hypocrite. You are like Diana's uncle, but you are worse. He, at least, does not pretend. You keep saying you have nothing against black people, but the words are empty. The truth is that you cannot accept that they are human beings exactly like ourselves, that they have the same hopes and the same fears and, like us, they hurt when you strike them.'

He leant forward in his chair towards his father. 'You are just like Jonas,' he said, 'who could build this house to the memory of his coloured mistress after she was dead, but who couldn't bring himself to marry her when she was alive. There is a new society in the making on this island at last, a society in which colour doesn't mean a thing, and you and Diana's uncle have locked yourselves out through your blind prejudices.'

He paused for a moment; taken completely by surprise,

Cleydon searched desperately for words to stem the bitter, unexpected tide of his son's anger; but David cut him short.

'I am going to marry Diana,' he said, 'and I no longer give a damn for your opinion on the matter. You look at her and you can see only the colour of her skin; when I look, I see someone full of love and hope for the future. I am truly sorry for you.'

For a full minute Cleydon sat there without replying. Then he rose to his feet, the blood pounding at his temples, his body shaking with an uncontrollable fury.

'Very well,' he heard himself say in a voice he scarcely recognised as his own, 'but if you marry that black girl you better know now that neither of you will ever be welcome in this house.'

David stood up without a word and went at once to his room. Cleydon was left alone on the verandah with the decanter of brandy and the two glasses which he had never filled. He was suddenly very cold, but he did not unstopper the decanter because he knew it was a condition the brandy had no power to cure.

At first light next morning, Cleydon heard from his bedroom the sound of David's car upon the gravelled drive; a door opened and shut, and then they were gone. In the silence that followed, he could hear the beat of his heart. On the table at the entrance to the hall downstairs, Lampit's niece had left a note for him:

'I am so very sorry that my visit should have brought unhappiness to you and David,' it read. 'If I had known, I would never have come. He loves you and it hurts him deeply. I want you to know that I understand how you feel about me. My uncle feels the same way about David. It is no one's fault; it is a consequence of our history. But isn't it sad that in your rejection of David's love for me and mine for him you and my uncle can find your only measure of agreement?'

She had signed it simply; 'Diana.'

13

Cleydon heard nothing from David or Diana for more than a year after that fateful visit to Illana's Hall. From a paragraph in the daily newspaper two months later he learnt that they had been married in a registry office in the capital. Scanning the list of guests present at the brief ceremony he noticed that Lampit had not been there either. Not long afterwards he read in the same paper that David had graduated with honours from his university and that he had taken a post with the Ministry of Agriculture, advising peasant farmers how best to develop their land. He was haunted by the unbearable thought that he had lost his son for ever.

At Illana's Hall he nursed his grief alone. Friends came round from time to time in a well meant effort to bring him comfort, but he could find no real pleasure in their company any more. After a while, sensing that they were unwelcome, they stopped coming. For the first time in his life, Cleydon began to seek refuge in drink; and all the time he was conscious of old Thomasina, crippled now by arthritis and a failing heart, hovering unhappily in the background, determined never to desert him.

One evening towards the end of that first year, she approached him as he sprawled in his chair on the front verandah, a drink in his hand, an unread copy of the day's newspaper across his knees.

'Massa Cleydon,' she said softly, 'you remember when you was a little boy I tell you 'bout de caterpillars on de frangipani tree?'

Cleydon nodded, recalling those brilliantly painted giants and his acute disappointment when he learnt that they eventually metamorphosed into nothing more exciting than clumsy, dun-coloured moths.

'Well,' said Thomasina, 'you remember how I tell you dat de colour don' mean a t'ing?'

'Yes,' Cleydon agreed. 'I remember.'

'Well, Massa Cleydon,' Thomasina continued, 'is de same wid Massa David an' his wife: de colour don' mean a t'ing.'

Before he could frame a suitable reply, the old woman had lost her courage and scuttled off again in the direction of the kitchen. Cleydon was left alone on the verandah with the company of his drink and his unread newspaper to consider, against his will, what she had said.

'The trouble is,' he heard himself say out loud after a while, 'it's too bloody late now anyhow . . .'

The first six months of the new year were the unhappiest of his life; more desolate, if that were possible, than the nightmare weeks which had followed Pat's death. Then, at least, he had had the comfort of his son. On the rare occasions now that he stepped out of the house, it was to walk alone into the hills behind the great white Hall, just as his grandfather Jonas had done in the dreadful evening of his own life. Like him, Cleydon felt that the pillars which supported his world had collapsed in ruins and that there was no hope of ever raising them again.

Occasionally, when he could thrust aside for a moment the curtain of his own misery, it occurred to him that Lampit, too, must be equally unhappy. He heard it rumoured that the man had publicly disowned the niece whom, for twenty years, he had cared for as his own daughter – the only human being, so it was said, that he had ever loved. Now he too knew something of what it was like to lose an only child.

In the middle of 1972, however, a general election was called in Saint Cecilia and, putting aside his personal grief, Lampit made his long-expected bid for political power. On the foundations of the trade union he had raised his own party and it was clear at once to everyone, from the content of his speeches, that his views had not mellowed with time. His party's platform was deliberately racist and, at his public meetings all over the island, he repeated over and over again his well-remembered promise: a black man's paradise in Saint Cecilia.

'Once we chase out de white man,' he declaimed to the people who came to admire his oratory, 'all de rest is easy.'

And always his speeches closed with that arrogant, ringing catch phrase which Cleydon had first heard with Pat that distant, nightmare morning in Victoria Square: 'Follow me, for I am de path to de future.'

It seemed to those who knew him best, however, that in spite of the old rhetoric a little of the fire had gone out of his delivery and that, in its place, there could be heard the faintest trace of self-doubt, as though he himself was no longer entirely convinced by the force of his own arguments.

Whatever the reason, on the day of the election the Cecilian people turned their backs on Lampit and what he stood for. Not one of his party's men was chosen for the Assembly and, in his own carefully nurtured constituency, he himself lost his deposit to a white candidate put up by the governing party. People, it was evident, had been willing to join his union because of the material benefits he offered, but not many had real sympathy with his political ambitions. The lesson was clear to everyone: Cecilians did not care to be divided any longer by the issue of race. The bitter past, they had decided, must be consigned to where it belonged. It was time to move on. David Langford had been right; from the cruel turmoil of three hundred years of history a new society was emerging in which the colour of a man's skin could no longer help or hinder him.

For the heir to Chaka's mantle it was a cruel blow. He was a proud man and he had convinced himself that he was a leader whose time had come. His public humiliation was complete. With a dignity that compelled a spark of admiration, he accepted the rebuke. He dissolved his party and the union from which it sprang and retired at once to the solitude of a small cottage in the mountains. As the sensation surrounding his rout died down, his name slipped out of the pages of the newspapers where it had once been so prominent. People forgot about him and his vision of a black man's paradise. In the new Saint Cecilia it was apparent that there would be room for everyone.

Some six months after those elections, Cleydon found in his morning post a letter from Diana. He recognised her writing at once. In spite of himself, his fingers trembled as he tore open the envelope.

'Our son was born last week,' the girl wrote, 'and we have called him Cleydon after his grandfather. He will be christened in the Queenstown parish church at 2 o'clock next Friday. He, at least, can have done nothing to offend you. Please come; and please bring Thomasina with you.'

It was Wednesday and crop time at New Providence, and Cleydon resolved to banish the letter from his mind by spending the day with his overseers at the factory; it had been a long time since he had done this. After an hour, however, he gave it up and returned unwillingly to the sanctuary of his study on the pretext that he wished to examine the estate account books.

The letter lay where he had left it on his desk; he took it up and read it through again. Once more he sought justification in his own mind for the stand he had taken with his son. His thoughts turned once again to his father and all the other West Indian members of his family who had preceded him. What would they have felt, he asked himself, had they known that the ultimate heir to all they had worked and suffered for was now to be the direct descendant of a coal black slave woman who had once toiled half naked in their fields with the Langford brand burnt deep into the flesh of her breast? And now he was being asked to put his own seal of approval on it all by attending the child's christening. The whole idea, he told himself, was unthinkable. He would have no part of it.

The dilemma would not be resolved, however, no matter how he willed it. When Friday came, he was awake before first light. He had spent the night agonising over his decision to ignore Diana's letter. He could eat no breakfast; he could only pace the floor of his study, aware of the sheet of paper lying on the desk, listening against his will to the upright clock in the corner relentlessly telling the minutes to two o'clock.

At half-past eleven, he was still resolved not to go. For the twentieth time that morning, he picked up the letter, read it once again and then flung it back upon the desk. This time, as he did so, his hand struck the framed photograph of Pat which had stood there since the day they were married. The picture fell to the floor; shards of glass splashed across his feet. He stooped at once to retrieve the photograph. Filled with contrition, he brushed the glass from it with the corner of his handkerchief. The face of his wife looked out at him from within the plain cedar frame, and in that instant all doubt and hesitation were swept away. He knew at once that she would have wanted him to be there. She had never shared his feelings about the need to keep separate black and white in the West Indies, and the child, after all, was her grandson too.

He flung open the door and yelled for Thomasina. The old woman came limping painfully from the marble hall where she had been keeping a kind of hopeful vigil.

'Put on your best dress,' Cleydon told her sharply, in an unsuccessful effort to disguise the collapse of his resolve. 'We are going to a christening and we have to leave in half an hour.'

She fled in panic without a word, tearing at the buttons of her starched white apron as she went.

By the time Cleydon hurried out to the Bentley thirty minutes later she was there waiting for him at the side of the car, sweating a little in the heat of the afternoon and wearing the same pink satin dress she had worn for David's christening more than twenty years before.

They climbed into the car; the wheels sent the loose gravel flying like birdshot from the surface of the drive all the way down to its junction with the metalled road.

In spite of Cleydon's best efforts, they arrived late at the parish church. He hurried with Thomasina into the cool gloom of the old limestone building, his eyes taking time to adjust to the soft light after the glare of the road outside.

Clustered around the font there was a small group of people. Among them, standing very close together, he could just make out Diana and his son. Cleydon ushered Thomasina into a pew and took his own place at the back of the congregation. The child, he saw, was cradled in its mother's arms, the delicate brown face almost lost among the white folds of the christening robe. As he watched, the child stirred and gave a robust, impatient cry; Diana bent her head and kissed the baby lightly on the cheek. The crying ceased. For one brief and fearful moment, however, the cry evoked for Cleydon a vivid mental picture of the child's great-great-grandmother enduring the kiss of the red-hot Langford brand. The palms of his hands were suddenly wet with sweat and he could plainly hear the beating of his heart.

Somewhere over to his right, he was aware that another latecomer had joined the congregation. Cleydon turned his head; sitting, like himself, some distance removed from everyone else, half screened from view by the dark shadow of a limestone pillar, he saw Lampit. For a brief instant their eyes met, but neither chose to give any sign of recognition. Well, Cleydon thought, the man was right after all: Massa's day is done; but at least they have named my grandson after me.

Then the ancient, pleasing words of the christening service filled the church and all attention passed to the child who was to be christened with his name.